T0123493

The
Anecdotal

William Bateman

authorHOUSE®

AuthorHouse™
1663 Liberty Drive
Bloomington, IN 47403
www.authorhouse.com
Phone: 1 (800) 839-8640

This is a work of fiction. All of the characters, names, incidents, organizations, and dialogue in this novel are either the products of the author's imagination or are used fictitiously.

Published by AuthorHouse 10/06/2017

ISBN: 978-1-5462-0951-5 (sc)
ISBN: 978-1-5462-0949-2 (hc)
ISBN: 978-1-5462-0950-8 (e)

Library of Congress Control Number: 2017915217

Print information available on the last page.

Any people depicted in stock imagery provided by Thinkstock are models, and such images are being used for illustrative purposes only. Certain stock imagery © Thinkstock.

This book is printed on acid-free paper.

A BRAND OF JUSTICE

Every Saturday morning, My kid brother Charles and I would go to Fishers Bakery for two loaf's of Day old bread, and about ten very small pies that went for about 10 cents. apiece, and if we had any change left over, we were to by a package of Motza's, (A jewish cracker that tasted good dipped in hot soup, and eaten.) Well, this one Saturday morning, Charles and I made our usual bakery run (As I called it).

Only, this Saturday morning would be a very different kind of morning. When we got there (It was only a longblock from our house), there wasn't the small line of peoplethere, that usually bought their day old bread on Saturday morning. There was no one there so, I figured that we must of gotten there early so, we stood there waiting for the door to open so that we could go inside.

Just as we were settling down for a wait, the door opened and a guy ran pass me holding a big Chocolate Cream pie in both hands.

And then three or four more guys ran pass me and Charles,

1

with a variety of pies in their hands and they all disappeared around the corner.

I stuck my head inside the store, and saw that the front of the store was empty. So, I rushed in dragging Charles with me, and racing into the rear of the store, I ran to the first Pie Racks that I saw, and grabbed four or five of the pies and raced back outside and quickly across the street and sat down on the running board of one of the cars parked there.

Charles soon followed, with a stack of pies in his hands. Where the bakery's personnel was, we never found out but, In our haste to grab pies, we didn't look at what types of pies we had taken but, I took off my muffler, and after wrapping it around the pies, I stuck them under the car.

After waiting for a few moments, we walked back across the street and went into the bakery.

This time we waited until the man came from the rear to wait on us.

We finally left the bakery with what we had gone there for, and then we made a quick stop to pick up our pies and leave that area.

Once we were about a half a block away from the bakery, we stopped and then I unwrapped the pies as we sat in the running board of another parked car.

After checking out the six pies, I found out that they were all Coconut Custard Pies. Knowing that we couldn't take them home, me and Charles ate a whole pie right there.

We started on another pie but, it was too much, and we

were now full to the brim with pie. So we gave the rest away, taking it slow in our walk home.

When we finally got home, we put the packages on the table and turned to leave.

My mother said, "Being's you boys went to get the pies and stuff without hassling me, I'm going to give you each a pie.

Clearing a place for us to sit at the table, she said, "Here! I'll get you both a glass of milk to wash it down with."

Me and Charles traded nervous looks, and he started to say that he didn't want any pie.

Not giving him a chance to say something incriminating, I sat him in a chair and we watched as mom placed a pie in front of each of us, along with a tall glass of cold milk.

Now it would seem that this was a normal happening in our house, our mother giving us pies and all. Well! It wasn't.

Usually she would say that we could have a pie after we had our lunch. And that was what I thought she would say but, I always get the idea that the fates has a lot to do with what happened.

After stuffing that small pie in with the pies we had already eaten, made us sick.

I was sick for two days from all that I had consumed, and Charles was sick along with me, we both were throwing up and had stomach aches, and the very smell of pie had me running for the bathroom.

I vowed that I would never do anything like that again,

and believe me! that the pie situation is one of the reasons I stayed on the right side of things.

I am now 76 years old, and since that event with the pies, I have never eaten another wedge or even a bite of Coconut Custard Pie since.

And I was only about fifteen years old when it happened, so I guess I learned my lesson, I played and I paid!

THE END

"BUSTED"

Mistaken Identity

My name is Bill'. and throughout my life, I've been in some pretty mean scrapes.

But! This tale of woe, is one that really happened to me when I was 14 or 15 years old.

One Saturday morning, when I was walking from my randmothers house at 180 Charlton St. to my own home at 197 Livingston St.

Which is within 5 blocks of each other, in the all black neighborhood, locally called the Third ward Newark.

As I walked along Belmont Avenue, I heard a siren and was jarred from my reveries by a squad car pulled up to the sidewalk, right where I was walking.

Two plain clothes men jumped out of the car and rushed up to me, and quickly handcuffed me my hands behind my back.

They never said a word, but guided me to the rear door of

the squad car. Where they opened the door and shoved me inside the squad car.

Getting back into the squad car, they drove me over to the thirteenth Precinct, and took me out of the back seat, and walked me quickly into the Precinct.

Once I was in the Precinct, they took me to a room, sat me down and one of the detectives said, "You drink Coke or Pepsi?" I said, "Coke!" and he promptly disappeared, his partner sat in a chair right in front of me, and said menacingly, "We're just about tired of hearing about your exploits Mosely, and we're tired of picking you up because you're too stupid to realize that these little petty crimes you're committing can only lead to your being Here in jail for some years of your young life.

"So! Tell me about your latest escapades?" When I started to speak, he said, "Look Boy! We have more important things to do, rather than baby sit you little Niggahs! So! Come clean, because, we already know what you've done. We just want to verify what you've done.

"So! It would be advisable that you confess, get locked up, And let us get on with more serious business."

I was scared out of my mind, and twice as angry because, I knew who these cops thought I was.

I also knew that they wouldn't listen to me, regardless of what I say so, I just sat there, looking angry, and not talking.

One of the detectives said, "Look Mosely, you might as well confess, because we already know that you did it."

I finally said, "My name ain't Mosely. It's Bateman! And I didn't do anything. But! If you'll call my mother, maybe we can clear this up faster.

The cops exchanged humorous looks and one of them said, "Sure kid! So what's your telephone number?"

I gave it to them, and one of them left the room and was gone for about five minutes, before I heard a loud voice coming through the door and knew that I was going to be going home.

My father was out there on the other side of that door, and when that detective returned, he handed me my coke, and they were gone for about another ten more minutes.

When they returned, they were giving me weird looks, and one of them said, "It's unbelievable!" The other cop nodded his head in agreement.

I looked at both detectives and said," What's unbelievable?"

The lead detective unlocked the shackle that held me to the table, and as I stood up, they both said, "Follow us."

When we stepped out of the room, I immediately saw my mom and dad sitting in chairs, their faces completely startled, as they gawked at the boy, manacled and standing between two other detectives.

As soon as I saw him, I shouted, "Ebeneza! What did you do this time?" And I made a beeline for him. the two detectives, stopped me, and one of them said, "Hey! Come On kid, simmer down."

Once the shock had worn off, the two detectives took me

over to where my mom and dad were sitting, and handed me over to them.

One of them said, "We're sorry that we put you through this but! Looking at both boys together in the same room, we're sure that you can understand what happened here.

My mom said, "Yes! We can see where you would make a mistake, But we would like to take our son home now."

The police were tripping all over themselves, more than willing to oblige my parents, and they ushered us out of the stationhouse as quickly as they could.

This was just one encounter I had with Ebenezer Mosely.

We just happened to go to the same grammar school and he got me into many encounters with the authorities. Plus he even played a role in parts of my personal life.

But! Those are different stories, for a different time.

The End

CHRISTMAS EVE

(A true story from: The Anecdotal)

You know! That old saying 'From the Mouth of Babes?' sure, those words don't carry a lot of weight.

What I mean, is that children can motivate grown-ups into doing either the dumbest things, or the smartest things, simply by the words that come out of their mouths.

But! Bad, Good, or otherwise, they do sometimes make us grownups pause for a moment and reflect, an example being:

About week and a half before Christmas of 1978, I heard (In passing), my oldest son Gilbert, who was all of seven years old, tell his little sister Yolanda who was five years old, and their baby brother Estevan, who was three years old, "Huh! There ain't any Santa Claus!"

Instead of interrupting them, I tucked that bit of information away in the back of my mind, vowing to deal with it later.

You see, Gilbert was easily led and I summarily thought

that some of his peers in school were trying hard to convince him that there simply wasn't any Santa Claus.

They were telling him that Santa Claus was their mother and father, because that was the only Santa Claus they ever knew.

When I heard Gilbert express his doubts to his sister and brother, I knew that I would have to do something to reinforce that special magic called Christmas back into his life.

And reinforce his attitude toward a holiday that he suddenly had doubts about.

So! Being the traditionalist that I was, I brought my wife's attention to the dilemma and we sat down each evening after the kids were asleep, and we formed a plan to bring Santa Claus firmly back into our son's mind, and reaffirm in him the spirit of the holiday.

So that as our oldest, he could he could help keep the magic in the minds of his little sister and brother at least for another year, and who knows, maybe spiritually for the rest of their lives. Each night after the kids had gone to bed, we sat down at the kitchen table and began building our plan, knowing that it would have to be fool proof.

It was hard to keep my patience for a week and a half because, holding my tongue has never been one of my strong points.

And seeing my daughter Yolanda slowly weakening as

Gilbert continued parroting the words of his peers, "Huh! There ain't any Santa Claus!"

And poor Estevan? Who! Looking up to his big brother, would believe anything that Gilbert said.

As Christmas slowly drew closer, and my wife and I had put the finishing touches on our plan, I felt confidence surge through me and knew that the plan would work.

Two days before Christmas, we bought a nice tall pine tree and with the kids help, we decorated it that evening, Gilbert constantly flashing me looks that said, 'You can't fool me Dad! I know that YOU and Mama are the only Santa Clause's who will be putting any presents under this tree on Christmas Eve.'

I smiled to myself as my wife and I exchanged secret glances, that said, "You just wait son, you just wait!"

Christmas Eve was spent down my Mother-In-Laws house but, we brought the kids back home early.

While they were out playing with the neighbor kids, we wrapped their presents and stashed them in the rear of our bedroom closet.

As evening fell, we called the kids in for dinner and as soon as they walked in the door, and were on their way to wash up for dinner, they were looking under the tree for presents.

When they saw that nothing was there, Gilbert said, "Where are all of the presents?"

As we sat down to dinner my wife said, "Oh! They won't

be here until Santa Claus brings them." Gilbert said, "Aw! Come on Mom! You know that there isn't any Santa Claus, You and Dad are . . . "

Yolanda, who was all of five years old cut in saying, "Yea! It's you and Dad!"

I said, "Santa Claus is listening and you' de better remember what he said about being naughty or nice."

After dinner and after the kids had taken baths, and amid loud protests, we put the kids to bed early saying that they had to go to sleep early or Santa Claus would pass up their house.

Besides, my wife said that I was going to bed because I had some chores that I would have to do the next day and for them to go to sleep.

That she would wake them up, when Santa was putting the presents under the tree, and that they didn't want to wake their father up because they knew how grumpy he could be if they wake him up.

While my wife went to her mothers house, and picked up the Santa Claus suit, I sat in the living room watching TV and listening to the kids move around in their bed, in their darkened room.

Ever so often, I would say, "OK YOU GUYS! CUT IT OUT IN THERE AND GO-TO-SLEEP!!!"

When my wife finally returned, she knocked on the door instead of just using her key and coming inside.

When I opened the door, there she stood, WEARING THE SANTA CLAUS SUIT. The wig of white cotton was slightly awry on top of her jet black hair, that was longer than the wig.

The mustache and the beard looked more like they were suffocating her and was larger than her face. While the plastic Santa Claus Suit made her look kind-a shiny and fat (And fat she wasn't).

She stood there for a frozen moment and finally said, "MERRY CHRISTMAS! HO- HO- HO."

In answer, I shushed her, and pointed to the now sleeping kids bedroom door, We both laughed at her antics quietly.

After she had shed the Santa Claus Suit and laid it on our bed, we went and gave the kids bedroom a quick check, and after a full day of activities, they were all asleep so! we put our plan into motion.

As my wife went to the closet to start putting the presents into a trash bag, I went as quietly as possible to our blanket draw in the hallway and took out an extra thick blanket, rolling it up she put it in the bed and pulled the covers up over it, shaping it into a body.

She then got one of her mannequin heads, the one that had the Afro wig on it and pulled one of my watch caps down over the hair.

Placing the head on the pillow (Away from the room) she pulled the covers up to it's chin. I draped my robe on the chair beside my side of the bed. While she was preparing the bedroom, I put on the Santa Claus Suit, with the nice plump pillow belted over my stomach.

Once I was dressed, we put the wrapped presents in the large trash bag outside the window, and I went out of the bedroom window (We lived in a one story complex).

I walked around to the front door with the bag full of presents slung over my shoulder and my wife let me in. As I went over to the tree, she turned off the lamps around the room and only the lights from the tree were left on.

As I began taking presents from the trash bag and placing them around the tree, my wife went and woke up the kids saying, "Be very quiet.

"Santa is putting the presents under the tree and if you're really quiet, I'll let you watch."

Right away Gilbert said, as they cautiously peeked into the living-room and saw a man in a Santa Claus Suit putting presents under the tree.

"Huh! Santa Claus is white and this Santa Claus is black So! I know that it can't be anyone but dad."

My wife looking slightly annoyed shushed him and said, "That is NOT your father! Your father is asleep in bed. Like I told you before, He has to do some extra work tomorrow and besides he came in pretty tired so, I told him that I would take care of everything while he slept."

Nodding his head negatively, Gilbert whispered, "Oooh! No! Mom! That's Dad right there by the tree."

My wife whispered, a note of anger in her voice, "You want me to prove that your father is asleep?"

They all chimed in, in hushed tones excitedly, "Yea!"

Without another word, my wife took them over to our bedroom door on tiptoes and cracking the door, she whispered, "Do you want me to wake him up? You know how he can be when ever you wake him up, making noise and all?"

Gilbert said, the note of assurance strong in his voice, "Well, you can let us see if dad is there because . . ."

My wife reached her hand inside the room, and locating the light switch flicked the ceiling light ON!

(Just long enough for the kids to see the sleeping form in the bed) and then OFF! plunging the room back into darkness.

She led them back to the spot they had been in watching Santa Claus. He was just finishing with the last of the presents and stood up, folding his bag.

Gilbert still had a skeptical look on his face as Santa Claus disappeared out of the front door.

I hurried back to the bedroom window and opened it quietly, once inside the bedroom, I took off the Santa Claus suit and stashed it in the closet along with the trash bag.

Putting on my PJ' s I put on my slippers and robe, pulling the blanket out of the bed and leaving it messy, I put everything in the back of our closet to be moved later.

I could hear my wife talking to the kids as they sat in the living-room looking at the presents. Pulling the watch cap down over my ears, I walked to the door, took a deep breath and flicking on the overhead light opened the door saying loudly, "What's all the fuss? What's going on?"

When the kids looked up and saw me standing there with my robe and night watch cap on, all of their jaws dropped and Gilbert was the first one to speak saying, "DAD! DAD! You missed it. We just saw Santa Claus."

Taking off my watch cap I scratched my head and yawned widely saying, "I've seen him before, many times. But! I thought I heard you saying that there wasn't any Santa Claus except me and mom."

He nodded his head no vigorously saying, "No! I take it all back. I SAW HIM! with my own eyes. Yolie and Estevan saw him too." Turning to them he said, "Tell dad! You saw him too didn't you?" They both nodded in unison, huge smiles on their faces and their eyes glowing with excitement.

My wife said, "OK You guys, hurry and go to bed so that you can get up early and open your presents."

She led them into their bedroom with me following. As she tucked them in, Estevan sat up in bed quickly saying, "Did you hear that?"

All movement stopped and we all looked at him, a question on our faces. He said in his piping voice, "I heard Santa's sleigh bells going away."

The night after Christmas, I sat the kid's down and said, "Santa Claus comes in many colors. Just because you see him on all of the Christmas Cards as a white man, you've got to remember that he is a spirit and can be any color he wants to be. You saw him as a black man because he wanted you to. But he can be any color at any time, always remember that."

Today, although Gilbert is Thirty-three years old, there's still a bit of that awe and magic left in his voice, whenever we recall that most glorious Christmas Eve.

THE END

DIEGO

The year was 1977, when my wife and I decided to move our family from Los Angeles, CA, to Albuquerque, NM. A move that I was looking forward to because, my esteemed mother-in-law seemed to be nosing more and more into our families business, I knew that we needed a change.

In January, 1977, we had three children. Gilbert Manuel: 6yrs, Yolanda Kym: 4yrs, Estevan Miguel: 2yrs.

And Trini was VERY pregnant, with our fourth child.

I had purchased an almost brand new Volkswagon Van with just 18,000 miles on the speedometer. I purchased it through the penny saver I picked up from one of those corner boxes that pass out newspapers and fliers and such.

I purchased the van from an owner who had just gone through a divorce and was in the midst of dismantling his home, and anxious to sell it.

Taking some leave from my job at the Veteran's Administration in Westwood, CA, and leaving the kids with our mother-in-law, we drove to Albuquerque, NM to get the lay of the land.

Once there, we found an area close to Kirtland Air Force Base (About five minutes away), and even closer to a Pre-school for our third son Estevan.

We decided that once we were settled in, we would try to find a parochial school for Gilbert and Yolanda.

We spoke to the manager of a small one story complex in the area and were shown an apartment that would be open by late August.

The manager said that he would hold the apartment for us once it was vacant.

Once my wife and I looked around the town and saw how beautiful it was, we were satisfied that this was where we wanted to settle.

We drove to the University of Albuquerque and the University of New Mexico during our travels around the town.

I checked out the Veterans Administration Office in the heart of the Business district and was pleased with what I saw. We stayed in a motel for a couple of days before we began the long drive back to Los Angeles.

Once we were back in Los Angeles, we went and picked up the kids from Trini's mother's house and returned to our apartment, and sat the kids down and told them everything that we saw in Albuquerque and they became just as excited as we were, although they didn't want to leave the friends and classmates they had come to know.

But! We were sure that once they saw the place, they would adjust and the past would quickly fade as they made new friends.

Meanwhile, Trini was growing bigger and rounder in her pregnancy. For a while, the doctors thought that she was going to have twins, and after we had estimated the length of the trip vs the rest of her pregnancy.

We knew that we would be cutting it close because, the baby was due the first part of September and we were leaving Los Angeles on the 22nd of August.

We were busy preparing for the move between June and August, and were ready to go on the 22nd of August 1977.

Staying in touch with the apartment manager, when our furniture was on its way to our new location by moving van.

When we finally left Los Angeles for Albuquerque, I knew that we had a long hard trip ahead of us, and even though Trini drove every once and a while to spell me, it was at a limited amount of the time because of her condition.

When we had driven for about five hours, we were tired and needed a rest, me from driving, Trini from tending to the kids, and the one she was carrying.

So, we decided to call it a day and settle into a Motel for the night, and Trini could lay down and rest her back, and get some sleep, while I took care of the kids, which would consist of all of us crashing because, even the kids were tired.

We could continue our trip the next morning fresh and with more stamina.

We found a Great Western Motel with a vacancy sign showing, and I parked in a slot out front. Leaving the kids in the Van, we went inside to register and, as we approached the desk, the desk clerk took one look at us and his whole demeanor changed from pleasant to one that said that a couple of strange animals were approaching his desk.

The clerk said quickly, "Eh! Can I help you?"

I said, "Yes! We would like a room with double beds. As you can see, we're pretty beat up and need baths, and a good night's sleep after the long drive from Los Angeles.

"We have our three children outside and as you can see, my wife is REALLY pregnant and we . . . !"

The desk clerk said too quickly, "We don't have any vacancies, we're all filled up, I'm sorry but, you'll have to go somewhere else, but that's how it is."

I stared at the clerk through tired eyes and started to say something but, Trini pulled my sleeve and in resignation turned tiredly away from the desk.

Following her out to the Van, I thought to myself, 'Huh! I should have busted that crackers face. Here I thought that that racism crap was finally over.

'(I'm black, and Trini is Hispanic) but, I see that it's alive and, well! I see that it's alive and doing very well.' But! too tired to argue and not wanting to get physical and start a rukus, I climbed back behind the wheel and noticed that the kids were all asleep.

After about two more hours on the road, we finally found a motel that would accept us. But by the time we found it, we were so tired, and Trini was having such bad pains in her back, that we didn't really care what the motel looked like, as long as it had beds, a shower, and a bathroom.

———ᘻ———

After a good night's sleep, we were all up the next morning, ready for some breakfast, and itching to get back on the road.

Once we all had our breakfast, we buckled into the Van and continued on toward Albuquerque.

About an hour into driving along a highway that was essentially empty of traffic, a strange thing happened.

We came upon a Semi-trailer truck hauling a load. I sped up and after checking that the road was clear, I passed it on the left and quickly got back into the lane in front of it.

I sped up, and after driving up and down a hilly area, we soon left the Semi far behind us.

What was strange, was that when I slowed down and just cruised along, I looked into my rearview mirror and saw that the semi had caught up with us on a level stretch.

Instead of passing us on the left and getting back in front of us, he seemed to be trying to pass us on the INSIDE!!! Which was to my right.

The semi's maneuvers were dangerous and life threatening

so, I sped up and when we came to a hill, I sped up the hill and again, we left the semi far behind us.

For a while, we saw no cars or anything, so the kids were soon taking a knap in their seats and Trini was laying in the back seat, wide awake but resting.

I drove on, not thinking about anything in particular but, when I looked into the rearview mirror, a bolt of fear went through me and I was immediately alert.

The semi was back behind us, and it was once again trying to pass us on the inside, on my right side. Fortunately, we came up on too many dips on the right side of the road so the semi had to stay on the road behind us but, every time we came to an area that was flat on my right hand side, he would have either turned in, and either pass us or run into us causing us to crash.

But, every time we came to those flat area's I would speed up and leave him far behind us.

We finally came to a very steep hill and taking advantage of the speed in which I could go up that hill, apposed to how slow the semi could pull it.

Once at the top of that hill, I didn't dare slow down but, continued driving at a high rate of speed for about two or three miles.

From that time on, until we came to the outskirts of the city of Albuquerque, we never saw that semi again, and believe me, I never wanted to, it was gone but never forgotten.

As we drove into the town, a sense of relief came over me

as I said to myself, 'The journey is finally Over.' and we were about to finally settle in and become our own family.

When we got to the apartment complex, and checked it out, we found it ready for us to move into.

Now all we needed was our furniture, which hadn't arrived yet so, we had to stay in a nearby motel for a couple of days.

Once the furniture arrived and we had settled in, I took Trini to the Kirtland Air Force Base Hospital, where she was examined and they opened a file on her, while sending for her files from the West Los Angeles VA Hospital.

We found a nearby Parochial School in the neighborhood and got Gilbert and Yolie on the waiting list.

We took Estevan to the nearest Grammar School and got him enrolled into a Pre-school class.

Albuquerque took us in and we became their own. It was a very beautiful city plus, we were close to every need that we could possibly have.

Everything was five or ten minutes away from our apartment. We had very friendly neighbors who welcomed un into the neighborhood with a pie and a casserole.

The following weeks were very busy as we got closer and closer to the date of our forth child's birth.

By the end of August, Trini was barely moving around and she looked like she was going to have a cow or something but, I had another problem.

I had gotten my wires crossed by not monitoring my job situation before we left Los Angeles.

I had quit my job at the VA being told by my immediate supervisor that I could take up where I left off bu getting rehired at the VA in Albuquerque it all sounded good at the time but, when I went to the VA in Albuquerque and found out that I would have to re-apply and wait a span of time for everything to be processed, plus they had a waiting list of applicants.

The turn-around taught me never to count on promises, but to check and double check to be sure that there was a position that goes along with the re-location.

Suddenly, I was up against it, with a baby coming, and our finances somewhat depleted, I now had to find a full-time or part-time job to help us with our finances until a slot opened up at the VA.

September the 11th, between 4:00 and 4:30 PM, Diego Matine, Hakan, Bateman came into this world, weighing 10lbs, 5 Ounces, 23 inches.

About fifteen minutes before Diego was born, I was in the waiting room, walking the carpet.

There was no one there except me that afternoon, But! suddenly, a very tall, very large, and beefy nurse came out of the delivery room, where Trini was having the baby.

She made a beeline over to where I was pacing. Seeing the look on her face, I wondered, 'What is she mad at me for. ' I retreated to one of the couches and sat down.

Towering over me, her fists on her ample hips, she stood

over me and glaring down at me, she said, "Are you Mr. Bateman?"

I nodded yes, and she said angrily, "Why aren't you in there with your wife? Supporting her through this ordeal?"

I shrugged saying, "No! That's alright! I'd rather stay out here and wait for . . . !"

Without another word, the nurse reached down and grabbed my shoulders, and physically lifted me up off of the couch, and over a small table in front of the couch and then to the floor in front of her.

She spun me around, grabbing me by the scruff of my neck and with a small push, propelled me into the delivery room, and over to the head of the gurney where Trini was reclining, and sat me down (Very hard) in a chair there.

She then walked over to the door leading into the waiting room and, with her back to the door, she just stood there, barring any way out of the room.

And crossing her arms, she just stood there glaring at me, daring me with her eyes, to try and leave.

Out of four of my children, Diego was the first one I actually saw born to my wife. And believe me, it was a mind boggling experience, one that I would remember all of my life.

I thought to myself, as the nurse wrapped a blanket around Diego's very loud voice and body, 'How could something so big, come out of such a little place?"

I was awed, joyful, and very glad that the ordeal was finally over because, I think I was feeling weaker than Trini.

The huge nurse came over to where I was sitting with our son in her arms and laying him down in Trini's arms, and looking at me, she said directly to me, "There! Now that didn't hurt at all did it?"

Suddenly her face broke into a warm smile, this way I knew that she wasn't going to squash me like a bug.

Trini stayed in the base hospital for three days while I took care of the rest of the kids while she was gone.

I gave them baths, I fed them, I dressed them, I took them to school, and picked them up after school was over.

I made sure that they did their homework, and kept an eye on them when they went out to play. Although, I was dying to get a job, being a part time mother was an experience that I won't ever forget, and it changed my whole attitude towards mothers staying home, while us men went to work.

When Trini finally came home, I had everything ready. The babies crib was right beside our bed, and with the kids crowding around it, while Trini got into bed. Boy! It was a day of wonder for them and it was a wonderful time, and one of great happiness.

As the weeks and months progressed, Diego seemed to be growing by leaps and bounds. It wasn't until about three months or so after his birth, that we discovered that Diego was diagnosed with Asthma.

Besides my not having any success at getting a job, this

was the only bad news to mar this period of our lives and finding this out was punctuated by our hearing him gasping for air in the middle of the night.

When we took Diego to the hospital for his checkup, we were told that when Diego reached the age of eight months, they would start him on a medicine called Somopholin to keep his lungs clear of fluid.

They warned us that this medicine would make Diego hyper but! It would also keep him well Diego was big for his age and very strong. He ate everything that passed his lips and was always curious and most of all, he was very loud.

Whenever he started crying, his voice would carry and could almost shake the walls.

The bigger he got, the stronger he got and he played rough, from the time he first started crawling. Here was a kid that was examining every toy he got, trying to find a weak spot that could help him destroy it.

He's the only kid I know who, at the age of one year, completely destroyed a Tonka Toy that was suppose to be indestructible. Diego was a boy wrecking crew.

When he was a year and a half, we came to what I call the fatal day. That morning, we took Diego to the Base Hospital for his checkup.

He was doing fine, breathing normal and a little hyper from the medicine but, we were happy with his progress.

His pediatrician sat with us observing Diego at play in a room full of toys.

As she watched him playing she said, "So! He seems to be doing well on the Somopholin!"

I said yes, and then she said, "Well! Diego looks very well infact, I'm going to prescribe that you double the dose. This way we can make sure that his lungs stay clear of fluid."

Trini and I exchanged a long look and I felt a sense of foreboding but, thought to myself, 'What the heck! She's the doctor, and I guess she knows what she's doing. '

So, that evening, once we put the kids to bed, Trini went into our bedroom and gave Diego his medicine, doubling the dose.

We stayed up watching TV and about an hour later, Trini went back into our bedroom to check Diego out. After a minute or so she called me into the bedroom saying, "Something's wrong with Diego."

I looked at Diego and saw that his eyes were wide open and his gaze was fixed and he wasn't moving at all.

A fear shot through me that I had only felt before when there was big trouble brewing. We asked a neighbor to watch the rest of the kids and bundled Diego up and took him to the Base Hospital.\

Once there, they admitted him right away and took him away. We were there for about a half an hour before we found out that they had four doctors working over Diego, and that he'd had a seizure.

After about an hour more of waiting, a doctor came to us

saying, "He's stabilized but, we are transferring him to the Hospital downtown.

"Where they have more sophisticated methods, and machinery that's needed for Diego's problems.

The doctor gave us a strange look saying, "What happened to make Diego have a seizure of this magnitude?"

The only thing that we could think of was that Diego's Pediatrician had told us to double the dose of Somopholin that we were giving him.

When we told the doctor this, he got really angry saying, "SHE SAID WHAT?"

We repeated what we had said and without another word, he turned and walked away from us, a look of death and destruction on his face, as he disappeared back into Diego's room.

A nurse came out of the room and told us that they were transferring Diego to the Downtown medical center immediately.

And that we could either ride along in the ambulance or follow in our car.

Trini went with the ambulance and I followed in the Van. After a short ride, we came to the Hospital and they had Diego into a room almost immediately after.

WE spent the next four or five hours waiting for some word about our son.

They now had about seven doctors working over Diego and that was one of a few times that I cried openly in my life.

I was scared out of my mind and we both felt that we were to blame because, if I had listened to my heart, and Trini had listened to her intuition, and not given Diego that double dose of Somopholin, Diego would have been fine.

Now, his life hung by a thread because of our stupidity. Man! We were really scared.

While we were in the small chapel they had in the hospital, Trini tried to comfort me, even while she feared, and we prayed together, only to both end up crying and clinging to each other, the fear a palpable giant even in that small chapel about 4:30 AM, we heard a bellow that filled the corridor and made my heart sing. We both recognized Diego's voice, and the doctor hurried out of the room, a smile on his face as he said to us, "Good News! Your Son is going to be alright!

He's been revived and . . . . Well! As you can hear, he's going to be fine. As soon as we quiet him down, you can go in and see him."

A nurse returned to us once they had calmed Diego down. She said, "Diego is now resting quietly, and you can go in and see him now. "

We went into Diego's room and there in a steel crib, lay our son.

He looked fine and like any other child looks when he or she is asleep.

They had a taped down IV in his tiny arm. He looked so vulnerable and our hearts went out to him. Realizing what we had put him through with our stupidity.

But! we also realized that hindsight could only serve to make sure that we didn't make the same mistake again. We vowed that we would be definitely getting a second opinion from that moment on. The Doctors said that Diego would be in the hospital for at least ten days for observation.

Well! If Diego had been the average child, there wouldn't have been any problem. But! As you'll see, Diego's stay in the hospital was anything but average.

After three days in the hospital, we knew that Diego was getting better because, when we went to visit him on that third day, he was asleep.

The only problem that I found on that third day was, they had tethered his arms and feet and his IV had been transferred from his arm and had been taped to his forehead.

And if you never saw a kid with an IV taped to his forehead, I'm sure you're among the majority, and will say never before. Well! it's not a pretty sight. Some thought that it was cute but, I wasn't amused.

The nurse explained that whenever they had put the IV in either of his arms, he would pull it out. So, in order to make sure that he didn't keep on pulling the IV out, they taped it where he couldn't see it.

When they woke him up, they took off the fetters. He crawled around in the crib and played with the toys scattered around and we stayed with him for as long as we could that day, and Diego never noticed where the IV was.

On our next visit, to our relief they had done away with the fetters.

But, then! We found that Diego was trying to climb out of the crib, and had been for some time. More than once the nurses had found him hanging by his hands, outside the crib by the horizontal bar.

In order to stop Diego, they finally put a top on his crib and now< he looked like he was in a gace.

The nurses told us that Diego was gaining strength on a daily basis and by the fifth day, we knew that he was back because, the nurses complained that when he found that he couldn't climb out of the crib because of the top that had been put on it, he got angry and shook the crib apart.

Another thing the nurses complained about was, that they had tried to keep Diego from taking naps.

Because, he had so much energy, that he would play all day, becoming tired late in the afternoon and then he would take a nap.

He would wake up before the evening meal and when all was quiet, late at night Diego would wake up and start crying.

And would wake up the whole nursery full of sleeping babies and they would all start crying. They had to have extra nurses on the baby ward incase Diego woke up, so that they could begin the task of quieting him when he did wake up, so that they didn't have to quiet down all of the babies.

When we finally reached the tenth day, the nurses were so glad that Diego was going home, that they ignored protocol, and when we came to visit him on that last afternoon, and get the Doctor to release him, we found him sitting on his diaper bag, dressed in his street clothes.

A tall slender nurse was standing beside him with her arms folded, with a resolute look on her face, just to make sure that he didn't wander.

Trini was furious because, we had been told by the Doctor, that Diego was suppose to be released at 4:30. PM And it was just 12: 00 Noon.

By this time, we were both working, and on our lunch breaks, the rest of the kids were in school, so we were caught in a bit of a dilemma because, we had asked to get off early to pick Diego up from the hospital but, not a half-day off.

As we were about to leave, Diego's Doctor happened to walk by, I guess on his way to lunch. And upon seeing Diego in his street clothes, and all of us heading out of the front door with Diego in tow. He called out to us, telling us to wait for him.

He said, when he caught up with us, and addressed his remarks to the nurse, who was walking us to the door, "What is this boy doing in his street clothes?"

Looking at my me and my wife he said, "And exactly where do you think you're taking him?"

The nurse started to say something but, the Doctor stopped her. He was livid with anger and he said in a firm voice, "How can you release this boy without ME first checking him out, and signing his release form?"

He said, "Who ordered his release?" The nurse told him that the head nurse had ordered it.

The doctor said, "Later this afternoon, I want all of you nurses pn that station to come to my office, I have some words for all of you.

"Right now! I'm going to lunch but! I want the child to be taken BACK!! Up stairs, put into a gown and placed BACK in his crib. I want this done RIGHT NOW!!"

As he turned to go, he stopped and said, "NO! Perhaps I'd better do better see to this myself. But! You!

You go back to your station and inform them of what I told you."

Lifting Diego in his arms, we walked to the elevator. As the four of us got on the elevator, the doctor was muttering to himself angrily.

We stepped off of the elevator at our floor and going to the nurses station, the doctor got Diego undressed and he checked him all over.

Finding him sound and healthy, he signed the release saying, "I'm sorry for the problem, there is no excuse for the nurses to act like that."

We told him that we were both on our lunch break and had to get back to work. We had asked to get off of work early and would have to get back to work and come back at three o'clock.

The doctor said, "Fine! Then we'll expect you at three o'clock." He smiled at Diego saying to us, "Please forgive that small lapse in protocol, it will never happen again. Ruffling Diego's hair, he stood there for a moment, and then he was gone.

We returned to the hospital at three o'clock and picked Diego up. When we got home, we sat drinking coffee and watching Diego putter around in his crib.

I suddenly broke out in laughter, that I just couldn't hold back any longer.

Trini said, "What's so funny?"

I said, "Do you realize that our son is the first and probably the only kid of his age, who has ever been evicted from a hospital?"

We were silent for a moment and then we both burst out laughing. And you can take this for gospel, everything I've told you really happened.

THE END

GUARDIAN ANGEL

(Life On The Streets)
1985-1986

Walking the streets of Long Beach, California for a year and a half, my residence being a local Dunkin Donuts shop, for the first three months there.

I ranged the Long Beach area questing for a job of any kind, and leaving applications in many different locations. My first day of homelessness in Long Beach almost ended in disaster, for that morning I was stopped by a tall, heavily muscled young man.

Glaring into my eyes, an intense look on his face, he said, "I'll tell you what my man, you get me two rocks, and I'll give you ten bucks."

Not being schooled on the drug culture, I puzzled over his request, and I tried to figure out why he would give me ten bucks for two ordinary rocks? Shrugging my shoulder's, I said, "Wait here! I'll be right back."

Going around the corner, I entered a vacant lot I had seen

as I walked down the street, and I searched out two of the smoothest, roundest small rocks I could find.

I rubbed the dirt off of them and walked back to where the young man was waiting.

I held out my closed right fist, while my left hand was opened palm up. He held out two fives in one hand and opened the other hand waiting.

I dropped the two small rocks into his opened palm and reached for the two fives. The young man stared at the two rocks in his hand for a long moment, and then glared into my eyes, saying angrily, "Mother %$&*(#@&! You trying to be funny?"

He shoved the two fives back into his pocket with one hand, and dropped the two rocks on the ground and reached for me, all in a few motions.

That guy chased me for at least ten blocks before he finally gave up, and it took me at least fifteen or twenty minutes to regain my composure.

Finding the Dunkin Donut at the end of my marathon run, I sat in a booth trying to sort out what had just occurred. It was in this haven that I learned from one of the guy's I met that day, about crack cocaine and learned the drill about being homeless.

While I still had a little money, I rented a PO Box in one of those Rent-a-mail box places, and called my Credit Union so that I could have my Air Force Retirement check mailed from there to my PO Box.

I went to the Greyhound Bus Station, and rented a locker to keep the few clothes and important personal papers I had with me.

I also went and opened a membership in the local YMCA; Which at that time was $10.00 Per Month, where I could take showers, and keep clean and workout.

And with the money I had left over, I found a Laundromat near my haven, where I could wash, dry, and iron my clothes.

After I had done these things, I hung around my haven, eating donuts and drinking coffee, and at least twice a day I would look for work. And I was constantly filing out applications and mailing them out.

Being an extrovert, it wasn't long before I had made quite a few friends within the clan of homeless, who nested in the haven.

While sitting in my haven, I began talking to the youngsters who always seemed to wander into the Haven off of the street, the ones that you knew didn't have by their dingy look.

Those kids, I would talk to and try to get them to tell me how they got there.

I would try to help them get jobs, or I even talked a few of them into going back home and giving it another try, once they found out what they were up against.

Right away I learned that by trying to help get some of these kids out of the streets and back with their families, I didn't have much time to think about my situation.

So! Not having to think about my troubles, at least four boys I met in the haven, I talked them into joining the Armed Services, one going into the Army, three of them going into the Marines.

These were boys that were at such major odds with their families that their families didn't want to take them back so, I got them to send for their birth certificates.

When they were ready to leave for Basic Training, I saw them off with the same message, "I guess this is it. Now! If I ever see your face around here ever again, before you're suppose to show up, I'll fix it so that people won't recognize your face for atleast a month."

They would just smile and get on the bus taking them to Camp Pendleton or wherever, that was the last time I saw any of them again.

As the days, weeks, and months passed, I walked all over Long Beach, trying to get a job. I never got a referral for a job or anything.

And the very few interviews, and the few jobs I did land, I quit after a few days because they were so nefarious (Wicked in the extreme), that I felt that if I had kept the jobs, I would have probably ended up in jail, for they were jobs that were dealing with shady deals and with Companies bilking the Federal Government out of lots of money.

All of 1985 was a bad time for me but, near the summer of 1986, came the crowning moment of my experience of being homeless.

Sitting in a Norm's Restaurant drinking what seemed like my hundreth cup of coffee, no money, no job, no food, and most of all, no more will. I felt like I was on my last leg, and felt like I would be in this situation for a very long time.

At about 2:30 AM, I sat there angry and in despair, looking through the plate glass window out at the semi-foggy morning stillness.

I was preparing to walk back down to the Haven, when suddenly, an old man walked into Norm's and without hesitation, walked directly to the table where I was sitting.

He sat down across from me and said, "You don't belong here, you'll have to leave. This! is not your place."

I looked around to see who he was talking to but, saw that there was no one in the restaurant except me and him. I said, "You talking to me?"

He nodded yes, and repeated his words as I gave him the once over. He had on a white suit, and white shoes, a white felt hat and a white overcoat.

His skin was a walnut brown, and he had dark brown piercing eyes, his hair was as white as was his thick mustache and he sported a cane.

After repeating his words again, he stood up and walked out of Norm's, leaving me sitting there wondering whether or not I was going mad.

I thought to myself, "Oh well! No doubt this guy is one of the nuts that I saw on the street sometimes earlier today."

So I shoved the incident into the back of my mind and walked back down to the haven.

Two days later, while I was going through my tote bag in the Greyhound Bus Station where I kept all of my important papers, I came upon two coupons from the New York Life Insurance Company.

Going back to the Have, I sat in a booth and sipped a cup of coffee while I perused the coupons.

I found that they added up to more than three hundred dollars and some change, that I could collect if I cashed them in.

Hustling up enough change to catch a bus to downtown LA, as soon as I got there, I went straight to the New York Life Insurance Branch building early the next morning, with the idea that I would cash the coupons in and live better for w while until I get a job.

When I got there, I rode the elevator up to the fifth floor of the high rise, my excitement rising with the elevator, and when I stepped out of the elevator on the fifth floor, I hurried to the door with the New York Life Insurance Logo on it and opened it, I walked into a quiet, busy office.

Fishing out the coupons, I stood at the counter waiting until a young lady looked up from what she was doing and asked if she could help me.

Holding up the coupons, I said, "I'd like to cash these coupons in."

Coming to the counter, the young lady took the coupons

and studied them for a moment before saying "If you'll wait for a moment Mr. Bateman, I'll get your agent, she'll handle this for you."

After another short wait, another lady came out of one of the rear offices and said, as she quickly scanned the coupons, "Would you step this way Mr. Bateman?"

I followed her into her office and sat down while she perused the coupons more closely. She finally said, "My advice to you is that you hold on to these coupons."

My anticipation of getting money that I could use right away plummeted as I said, "Look! Doesn't it say on those coupons that I can cash them in, and get three hundred dollars and change?"

She said hesitantly, "MMMmm! You shouldn't do that because, if you do, you will close out your policy, and you don't want that to happen."

Angrily I said, as I saw the three hundred dollars slipping further, and further away, "Whoa! Look lady, just give me the money, never mind the rest, I'll deal with that later but, right now, I need the money."

My agent gave me a long look saying, "Wait! Let me try a few things before you make up your mind OK?"

Before I could say anything, she got on the phone and was speaking to someone on the other end in low tones.

After she hung up, she smiled and said, "Mister Bateman, do you have a bank or Credit Union that you do business with."

I said angrily, "Bank? What would I need a bank for? After all, it's only three hundred bucks we're talking about right? Why would I need a bank?"

She said, still poised and in control, "What about a Credit Union? Do you belong to a Credit Union?"

I said, "Yea! I belong to a Credit Union but again, why would I need a Credit Union for such a small sum of money? That doesn't make any sense."

Still not understanding, and still angry, I said, "Why? Why all of the . . . all of the . . ."

My agent said, "Because Mr. Bateman, first of all, we don't have Five Thousand Dollars in this office to just dole out to you, So! If you'll give me the name, Address, and phone number of your Credit Union, I will call them right away and have the money put into your account."

I sat there on the edge of my chair, stunned and shaken to my core, as I got out my wallet and fished out my Credit Union Card. Handing it to her I said, "But! But how? . . . ."

My Agent handed me a sheet of paper that she had been typing, as she spoke to me saying, "Now! I'm calling your Credit Union and if you'll sign this release, I'll have it in the mail this evening and you'll be Five Thousand Dollars richer within ten days."

I signed, still not really understanding what was happening to me. The shock left me numb. I left the office, my coupons in my wallet and almost in a trance. I still couldn't believe what had just happened.

Once I got back to Long Beach, I went to check my P.O. Box, and found that it was full of letters and fliers.

Taking the mail to the Haven, I sat in a booth sorting out the fliers from the letters and found that I had four letters from companies that I had left applications with.

Again I was stunned because, this was the same day I had learned about the money. The letters gave me dates when and where I should go for my interviews. I was overjoyed and had to sit there for a moment and take in all that had happened to me.

The next day, I was walking down Long Beach Blvd. and walked pass a place I had been passing nearly every day that I had been in Long Beach.

I had always noticed a crowd of men and women there so, on this afternoon, I decided to walk inside and see what was there. I found out that it was a Government funded work placement area.

They hired the homeless men and women to work in the Southwest Marine Shipyard on Terminal Island, CA.

Getting paid on a daily basis, I could go to work the next day once I signed up. So, I signed on there and begun my slow rise from the abyss I had been living in.

I attribute my successful rise from the ashes to that early morning visit when I was sitting in Norm's Restaurant at my lowest point, and that strange man walked in, sat down at my table, and said those cryptic words.

My whole life changed AFTER that man's appearance.

And it seemed that my life was being guided by decisions that were made FOR me after that visit.

That morning I had lost all of my faith in just about everything but, after that day, I truly believed that God was guiding my life and my Guardian Angel, with his appearance, the course of my life changed. But this didn't deter me from trying to help people.

When I first got my job at Southwest Marine, I was earning $20.00 per day, and was still waiting to receive my windfall from my Credit Union and New York Life.

With my $20.00 a day, I either had enough to sleep in a fleabag motel, or enough to eat a good hearty meal, I didn't have enough money to do both.

I started at Southwest Marine at the very bottom, scraping barnacles from the bottoms of barges and ships.

To being a sand hog, and to cleaning out tanks in ships that had docked for repairs.

When I thought that I would never rise above the jobs I was getting, I caught a break and was made Lead Man of a new department called fire-watch, along with another guy named Willie Holley, our bosses name was Wayne Caley.

This new job put us in charge of fifty to one hundred men a day. These men were assigned to all of the ships that docked in Southwest Marine.

As lead-man of the fire-watches, Willie and I assigned these men to the area's where the welders, Pipe-fitters,

Electricians, Braisers, Etc. and whenever a fire started from their torches, the fire-watch was there to put it out quickly.

Willie and I also made sure that there wasn't any accidents and that our men had the proper fire extinguishers or anything else they needed to do their jobs.

Willie and I rotated working the ships one week, and one week working the office as Lead men. Due to the fact that there was no Union at Southwest Marine, and we sometimes worked overtime as fire-watches, substituting as Fire-watches on some of the ships after duty and getting overtime we could end up with from $500.00 to over $1,000.00 a week.

But! Before all of that happened, I was only making $20:00 a day working in and around ships that were jobs that most guys wouldn't do today.

But, even then I would help people wherever I found them.

One day near noon, on a day off from the Shipyards, I was returning from a visit with my kids in East Los Angeles back to Long Beach on the bus. Among the passengers on the bus, there was a young couple sitting in the seats in front of me.

They were cuddling and kissing and speaking to each other in low tones.

I just happened to be sitting close enough to them to strike up a conversation with them, while talking to them I noticed just how much younger the girl was, than her boyfriend.

When the bus stopped on Long Beach Blvd, some of the passengers got off, as did those two lovers and me.

I went back to my haven and while I sat there wondering whether I would go and get me a good meal or a flea bag motel.

I decided to get some sleep that night so, I hustled around and while I was waiting for the sun to set, I managed to stuff myself with donuts and coffee.

Then I hit the streets looking for a cheap motel and as I hurried along Long Beach Blvd and, looking at my watch I saw that it was One O'clock in the morning. So I hurried along and when I walked pass the Welfare Office, I came to a huge block of cement.

Sitting on top of that block of Cement was the same young girl that I had seen on the bus. I stopped when I got closer to her and saw that she was crying.

Looking up and down the empty street, I said, "What are you doing here?"

When she didn't answer, but kept on crying, I said, "Where is that boy I saw you with today?"

She stopped crying long enough to say, "I don't know! He told me to wait for him and left me here, where I've been waiting every- since."

My first thought was to get her some place safe, so I said, "Well! You come on down from there and come with me, I can't leave you out here where just anybody can do anything to you." I helped you down from the block of cement and we walked up the street until we came to a decent motel.

Once I got her signed in, I took her to her room saying

once we got there, "OK! I've gotten you a room and you can get some sleep but first, lets get something to eat."

The Motel was a true fleabag Motel, but the room was $15.00 per night. And it was just some place to stay for the night.

I took her to the nearest burger joint and she ate.

By then I was at the end of my $20.00 so, after she had eaten, I took her back to her room and said, "You stay here and don't worry, we'll talk about what you'll do about your situation in the morning. In the meantime get some sleep."

She looked at me as I walked toward the door and said, "BBBbbut! Aren't you going to stay here with me? I know you didn't do all of this for nothing, so what do you want?" The last was said with a slight tremor of fear and anticipation in her voice.

I turned at the door and said, "Look! You forget you said that. I'll see you in the morning, Now! lock the door behind me OK?"

I waited outside the door until I hear her lock it and walked down to the Haven, which was opened twenty-four hours, and was always packed with the most interesting people.

The next morning, I knocked on her door, not really expecting her to be there but! To my surprise, she opened the door, looking like she had just awakened.

I said, "Am I too early? Do you need more sleep?

You've got until noon you know."

She nodded no, and let me in, to wait while she took a shower and dressed. After getting her a hearty meal with money I had borrowed against my next-day's paycheck.

As she ate, I said, "Now! After you've eaten, you can call your parents and tell them that you're coming home."

She started to protest but I said, "Uh! Uh! I don't want to hear it. Or do you want to end up where I found you this morning?

And suppose I hadn't been there to bail you out? You could have ended up in a very bad situation."

She said, "My mom and Dad are mad at me, and besides, we don't get along."

I said, "Maybe! If you give them a chance, they'll give you a chance, but either way, you'll have to work that out between you and them.

I gave her a quarter and said, "Now! You call your mom and tell her that you're coming home. I'll be right behind you to make sure."

Once she called, and I made sure that she was talking to her mother, I waited with her for the bus, and while we waited, I said to her, "I don't want to see your face around here anymore.

"If I do? I'll ignore you and then you'll find out what being mistreated means because, just like that guy yesterday, those people don't care about you and they will use you up like tissue paper and throw you away.

When the bus finally came, I watched her as she boarded it. I waved at her when the bus pulled out and surprisingly, I never saw her face in Long Beach ever again.

She might have gotten off before she got out of Long Beach or she could have stayed on it until she got to LA, She couldn't have been any older than fifteen, and I would like to believe that she had enough brains to know that she was in over her head out there in the streets.

I will never know but, I would like to believe that the one night on a block of concrete was enough to convince her to stay at home and stay safe.

Think about it, once I met that old man; Whom I will always consider as my Guardian Angel, my life took a turn for the better and eventually, he led me from the Dregs of the street, into the arms of prosperity.

And even while I was in the midst of the chaos that was my life in the streets, I was led to people who needed help, and a way out of their bad situations, I think you know the results of my giving aid.

THE END

LOBSTER FEST

Folks! Do you remember that old saying that the truth is always stranger than fiction? And so it is with this short story. But! I'll let you be the judge of that.

While I was Stationed at Mt. Hebo Air Force Station, on top of a mountain, in Tillamook Oregon, which was a Radar Site along the Dew Line.

After being stationed there for six months, NCOs were allowed to move into the town of Tillamook.

When I received permission to move into the town, I hustled to find an apartment to move to. After looking around, I finally found an apartment complex that had a one bedroom apartment to let.

I moved into the apartment on a Sunday and once I had the apartment arranged, I was sitting at my kitchen table making a list of the things I would have to pick up from the store down the street.

Due to the fact that I had barely moved into the apartment, when the knock came on my door, I was surprised but, I opened the door and there in the hallway stood a man holding a big bucket full of water.

I said, "Can I help you?"

The man said, "I would like to welcome you to the apartment. There are quite a few of you Airmen moving into the community, and we want to show that we welcome you guys."

I said thank you, as I watched him sit the large bucket on the floor and say, "I want to present you with this." and he pointed to the bucket.

I looked at the bucket and thought, 'Huh! This guy must be joking. Who gives somebody a bucket of water as a gift?'

I thought that because I was black, he was trying to be funny and started getting angry.

But, movement in the bucket caught the corner of my eye and I said, "Eh! What's in the bucket?"

The man smiled saying, "Lobster! Fresh caught this morning. I just thought that since I had a couple of extras, my family and I would like to share them with you.

I smiled saying, "Thank you. I really appreciate that."

The man said, pointing at the bucket, "When you're finished with the bucket, we're in apartment 12. Just knock on the door and leave it."

I thanked him again and closed the door, looking suspiciously at the bucket.

The water was almost to the top of the bucket but now, when I looked directly into the bucket, I could see The motionless lobster, which turned out to be two of the largest lobster I have ever seen before in my life.

And I was immediately struck by their color. Being from the heart of Newark, NJ. This was the first time I had ever seen a lobster that wasn't already cooked, and I really didn't know anything about lobster.

But, I sucked it up, and said to myself, "Ah! You fraidy cat, don't worry, the things are dead, and all you have to do is probably stick them in a pot and . . . . ! boil them? Or do you fry them?"

Me and my idea's, I decided that I was going to fry them. So I broke out the only skillet I had, and filled it with oil.

I turned the burner on low, and decided that I would wait until it was bubbling before I put one of the lobsters in it.

So I sat down for a few minutes, watching the news on TV and when I heard the oil popping, I went over to the bucket and stuck my arm into the water and latched on to one of the lobsters and pulled it out of the bucket.

When I had it out of the water and was holding it in my hand, I realized just how big it was.

It just hung there limp in my hand so I hustled it over to the stove and started to stick it in the oil.

I guess it woke up when it heard the popping of the oil or just woke up but, it began snapping it's claws and moving around in my hand.

Scared out of my wits, I dropped it on the floor and ran

and got the broom out of a corner because, that was the only weapon I could find right away.

I grabbed the broom and ran back to where the lobster was wiggling and thrashing on the floor. I began beating it with the broom, and pushed and poked it around the floor.

Once I regained my senses, I got the mop and with the handles of the mop and broom, I finally got that monster lobster back into the bucket.

And I challenge anyone to even try to get a pissed off Lobster back into a bucket full of water with a broom handle and a mop handle, I dare you!

Once I got the lobster back in the bucket, I moved the bucket over near the door and mopped up the spilled water and just rested for a minute, eyeing the bucket angrily.

Finally, out of sheer helplessness as to what I should do, I called one of my buddies and told him what had happened. He said, "Don't do anything! I'll be right there."

We hung up and about twenty minutes later, he came over to my apartment.

He said, "NOW! What happened?

I told him and he stood up and walked over to the stove. Looked down at the skillet with all of that oil in it. He turned to me saying, "And what is this?"

I said, "What! I was going to fry me up some lobster. So what's wrong with that?"

He looked at me, with shock on his face and said, "Are

you nuts?" Shaking his head he said, "Look! Get out your biggest pot."

I got the only big pot out and filled it with water and he had me pour the oil back into its container.

Once the water was boiling, he took the lobsters out of the bucket and put them into the now bubbling pot of water saying, "No wonder that lobster had a fit. Man! You don't fry lobster, you boil it. And until it turns red, it's not dead. I said, "I found that out in spades when I picked up one of them. Man! It scared the hell out of me."

My buddie laughed saying, "Man! I sure wish I could have seen you try to get that lobster with its big claws back in that bucket with a broom handle and a mop handle." And he laughed.

I knew that I would hear about this again so I didn't even try to get him to stay mum about it. I knew I'd get it when I went back up on the mountain.

He said, "SO! Are you going to eat the lobsters after they are done? If not!"

I said, "Sure! You take them with you, but bring back my pot. I guess I lost my appetite during the battle."

When I took the pail back to my neighbor, I didn't tell him what had happened. I just thanked him for bringing them to me.

THE END

RUTH BROWN

The Big Fight
A Short Story

Today, if kids fight on school grounds, their parents are either sued, or the kid is kicked out of school for maybe, a week or so.

Today, everything has to be politically correct, and kids are more protected than ever, or than should be.

If they are threatened with a fight from one of their peers, they tell either the principle or their teacher, and the kid that was supposed to have threatened them, (Whether true or not), that kid is either sent home, or stay after school in detention.

Back in the day (1930's and 1940's), being sent home, or staying after school, this would only happen when the two were caught fighting by teachers, or the culprits were found out, by someone telling either the teacher, or the principle.

But! Actually, these two bodies, knowing that they had

more important things to deal with, would ignored the rumors of fights.

And sometimes the fights, knowing that if they broke it up, it would be only postponing the inevitable.

And besides, interfering would become their daily chore, and They had better things to do with their time.

So! Knowing that this would always happen, the kids would schedule their fights to occur after school, off of school turf.

Well, I happened to have a bit of a run-in with a girl, when I was in the sixth grade of grammar school.

And believe me, it was a run-in that taught me to forget about the off-handed way, that girls fight, or admit that there are some girls that don't stick to the rule of fighting like girls.

The day of this happening, (The fight), and you must remember, that back in the day, things were not so cut and dry, as they are today.

Back in 1939, if kids got into fights, usually in a locale far away from the school grounds, they had to finish that fight either victorious, or defeated, rarely would they fight on school grounds.

But! Sometimes (Like that time), you got so mad, you agree to fight anywhere.

And that's what happened In this case. If you won, you would have bragging rights for about Fifteen minutes. If you lost, then you would have your Fifteen minutes of scorn, from the kids you hung out with, Or the kids in your class.

But the episode would be forgotten almost as soon as it had occurred, and the kids would wait for the next incident that would spark another fight over something equally as stupid.

Well! The morning of my first encounter with Ruth Brown, I was a hall monitor, at 18th Ave. School.

I was stationed outside the school at the Northside Door, deterring students from entering after the last bell had rung.

I was to tell the late students that they were late, and that they would have to go around and enter the building through the front door, where they would be recorded as being late, and would get detention.

On this morning, I was at my post, and a girl named Ruth Brown approached my door saying, "I'm a little late, but if you'll let me go in this door, I'll be able to get to my class anyway, and it will save me the time I need getting to my class.

I looked at her and shaking my head no, I said, "No Way! You're going to have to go around to the front door.

"You know the rules, after the bell rings for the last time, no one goes in through any other door, except the front door."

After giving me a glaring, hateful look, she said angrily, "OK! Then I'll see you after school, because I'm gonna beat Yo! Ass!!"

With those choice words, she turned around and marched around the corner to the front door.

I was astonished by her threat, but never gave it a second Thought.

Now! Everyone knew Ruth Browns reputation because, she had a reputation of beating up girls and had the reputation of being one tough cookie when it came to fighting.

I had never seen any of her fights, and if I had, I wouldn't have been as smug about fighting her as I was.

In fact, I would have just let her sneak in my door, and that would have been that.

But! Looking at her, I saw a girl who was a little taller than me, but thinner than me.

I felt like I could beat her without any trouble so, I told my Main friends about the up and coming fight, all the time feeling that she wouldn't show up, After all, she was a girl.

And like magic, soon word of the coming fight, had spread all over school.

The closer we got to 3:15, the more I felt like she wouldn't show up, so by 3:15, when the bell rang and all of the doors opened to a flood of students raring to break free of school, for another day.

This day, instead of the flow of children being a haphazard rush for freedom from their classes, a lot of the students went to the side of the school furthest from the front doors and the main Office.

I got there first with my friends, and after taking off my sweater, and folding it up neatly, and handing it to my best friend Billy Boy, I just hung out with my friends, not really believing that she would show up.

Just when I was deciding that she wouldn't show up, and was about to walk away, who should walk around the corner? Ruth Brown.

And she came with a mean, business like look in her face, and mayhem in her body language without speaking to anyone, or actually paying anyone any attention, she took off her sweater, and after folding it up, she placed it on top of her schoolbooks.

I had stepped into the circle that had been formed by the crowd and when she stepped into that circle, it was on.

That girl put up her dukes, and instead of giving me the wind mill affect that girls usually did, she squared off and fell into a fighters pose.

When I saw that, I knew that I was in the wrong place.

But it was to late to turn back, and I went into my fighters pose and after making a couple of weak passes at her, I charged her and then the fight was really on.

All I can remember about that fight, is that this girl hit me everywhere but on the bottoms of my feet, and I can't be sure that she didn't hit me there a few times.

And me? Huh! I never got one shot in on her.

I was as serious as a heart attack, but nothing I did worked and once I saw that she was much quicker than I was, and after she had totally punched me out, I decided that I had enough of that girl, and I had done all that I could do. So! I turned around and ran for home. The jeers that following me loud and clear, I totally ignored and kept on running.

When I walked into the second floor apartment we lived in, I Was demoralized and beaten up and really hurting, both my face and my ego had been bruised.

I felt that I couldn't let my parents, especially my dad, know that I had been beaten up by a girl.

But! My mom took one look at my face and said, "What Happened to you?"

I said, trying to be nonchalant, "I got jumped by a couple of guys' After school. But! Don't worry, I got in my licks."

Just about that time, my brother buddy walked into the Kitchen from outside.

With a devilish smile on his face he said, "Hey Willie! Here! you left that fight so fast, you forgot your sweater. So I figured that I'd better bring it home for you, before somebody stole it.

Coming over in front of me, he picked up my face with a couple of fingers and said, "BOY! She really put some wupp on you didn't she?"

I was so mad, that I forgot where I was and said, "Did you know that she didn't fight like girls always fight? If you did, then why didn't you tell me ahead of time?"

Buddy smiled and gave me a look, and said, "I saw her fight once before and, yes, I knew that she fought like a boy, heck! She's a tom boy so! What do you want from me?"

My mom broke in saying, "Ah! So! You got wupped by a girl?"

Feeling caught up in my own lie, I nodded my head yes, Snatched my sweater from buddy and ran into the bedroom I shared with three brothers.

My brother buddy was in the seventh grade and was now going to Junior High School.

And I knew that he would probably give a blow by blow description of what happened, at the dinner table that night.

So! I decided that I'd better fess up now, since the cat was out of the bag, so to speak, and mom already knew what happened thanks to my big brother.

So I told my mom what really happened, and was surprised at her being sympathetic to me.

She cupped my chin in her hand and said, as she viewed my face for the fourth or fifth time, "Hmmm! She really did a job on you.

"But! Sometimes, you have to give someone a break, instead of getting broken. This time, you got broken, well the next time, if there is a next time, I'm sure you'll know what to do.

As you can imagine, I was the talk of the kitchen table that night.

As with most things, that situation disappeared as all situations do, when you're a kid.

When I saw Ruth Brown again, she was on time for school, and I'm sure that she came through the door I was watching just to remind me of that fight, and that I should let her alone.

Which I did whole heartedly agreeing with her.

That was one of the very few times I fought a girl, but I learned one thing, that all girls are not the same.

And just because a guy is stronger and rougher, and maybe even bigger, some of the girls are pretty tough.

Some of them are just as strong, and just as rough and tough as guys are, and you better not sell them short.

Because, if you do, you'll come away from a beat down with a girl, with a fat lip, a fat eye, and maybe a few teeth missing. But! That was back in the day, things have totally changed since then, haven't they?

The End

THE HORSE

Mothers! Imagine this! Your son bringing home a horse! A Living! Breathing! REAL LIVE HORSE!

And if you can, then you must live on a Ranch or something. But! For this to happen in the middle of a City, where there's no such a thing as space?

I think that would be another story, especially when you lived on the second floor of a three story apartment building, smack dab in the middle of the Newark, NJ's Black Community, called the third ward.

Sounds kind-a Impossible? Well! There's no such a word as impossible where my son Willie is concerned.

It all started on a Saturday afternoon, while I was preparing dinner. Being a woman, you know how it is when you're cooking.

Naturally, you don't want to be bothered by your kids running in and out of the house with lots of banging and yelling, telling a lot of tales when you try to stop them and ask what's wrong with them.

Well! That afternoon, as I was cooking, I noticed (Out of the corner of my eye) Willie trying to slip unnoticed from the kitchen into his bedroom without disturbing me, and that was this boys particular style.

He looked hot, tired and very worried about something.

When I stopped him and could hold him still long enough to ask him what was wrong, that's when the impossible became possible.

That was the beginning of what was to turn out to be the beginning of a nightmare. If I had known what was going to happen, I wouldn't have asked him any questions at all. I would have simply ignored him and let him continue on into the bedroom, although that would have only delayed the events that followed just a little.

But! Being a concerned mother, and not a seer, I asked him, "What's wrong with you boy? Why are you trying to sneak around here?"

He looked up at me, his eyes filling with ready tears, as he said, "Mama! I found a hossy, can I keep im?"

Well! Willie only being ten years old was prone to exaggerate and not wanting to seem extra hard on him I said, "Sure, you can keep it. You found it didn't you? So what's the matter? One of the boys downstairs trying to take it away from you? Here! Let me see it."

I reached out my hand, thinking that he was talking about a little plastic animal.

When he just stood there crying even harder, I could feel

my patience draining away, when he said loudly, "I Can't Mama, it to big."

I stood there puzzling over his words, when it dawned on me that he wasn't talking about a toy, he was talking about a REAL HORSE.

Now my children (I have three boys and one girl), have over the years brought home all sorts of animals at one time or another and would talk their father and me into letting them keep whatever the animal they asked for.

Whether it be Cat, Turtle, Garden Snake, but mostly Dogs and Cats. The understanding was, that they would tend and clean up after whatever animal it was at the time.

For a moment I was stunned and couldn't believe my ears. I said in quiet awe, "You FOUND a real . . .

Live . . . Horse?" I just stared at Willie as he jumped up and down in front of me saying, "Yes Ma'am, I Found im, can I keep im? Please Mama? I take care of im, an feed im an all."

Still not wanting to believe what my intuition told me was true, I cupped his chin in my hand, held his face up and looked deep into his dark brown eyes, while I dried his tears with the edge of my apron, saying, "You Found a horse? A real live horse?

Boy! Now where would you find a real live horse in the middle of THIS city?"

Willie said, "I found im down the street, standin by the sidewalk."

I let go of his chin and turned back to the stove to check

on the roast that was in the oven, so that he couldn't see how flustered I was, saying over my shoulder angrily, "Well! You just take him back where you found him." In a sense, I still didn't want to believe him.

When I stood up and turned back around, he was still standing there, so I put my fists on my hips and gave him my special backside warming look and said, "NO! YOU CAN'T KEEP NO HORSE! AND THAT'S THE END OF THAT!"

Turning back to my cooking I said over my shoulder, "Huh! There ain't hardly any room in this apartment for all of us, no less a horse."

You see, I was still halfway wanting to believe that he was just exaggerating, like he sometimes did.

And I was on the verge of running him out of my kitchen when he burst out crying again.

A sudden fear welled up in me as he said loudly, mouth wide open, all of his teeth showing, tears flowing, "Mama! I can't take it back, I jus can't."

I gave him another one of those hot looks and said, "Now don't you keep up that crying, you hear me? You can't have no horse and that's the last I want of it.

"Now! You take that horse back down the street and you it where you found it."

Well. that boy just kept on crying and was now backing away from me, his eyes glazed with fear as he said, "I can't."

I was at my last bit of patience and said, "What do you

mean you can't? And why can't you take him back where you got him from? And stop that crying boy!"

Willie stopped crying quickly and wiped his eyes on his shirt sleeve, and with his face screwed up, he said, "Well, I can't take him back."

Suddenly, I heard strange loud noises coming from the hallway. I said, trying to ignore the sounds, "And just why can't you take him back?"

He said, a look of fear still on his face, "Well cause he's kind-a stuck in the hallway door, or was the last time I saw im."

Pointing to the chair beside the cabinet that held my special china, my heart now quaking in my chest, I said, "Boy! You sit down in that chair and don't you move.

I'll tend to you later, after I find out what you're talking about."

When I opened the kitchen door, I heard a whinny of pain float up the stairway, along with a crash of hooves on the floor of the hallway, and from the second floor on up, the neighbors were in the hallway, curious about all of the noise.

I thought to myself as I looked down the stairs, my heart in my mouth and a sinking feeling coming to my stomach, 'Well I can forget about that boy exaggerating because, most of the time liar and devil that he is, of-course, he couldn't be lying this time.'

When I knelt on one knee, and got a better view of the front door of the building. There! as big as life, whinnying in pain, his horseshoes clumping loudly against the wooden floorboards of the hallway, stood the biggest, ugliest plug (work horse) I'd ever seen before in my life, and it was definitely stuck in the doorway.

From what I could see, his stomach had bloated well past the door frame on both sides and his screams of pain which were getting louder, had drawn a sizable crowd of onlookers outside the doorway from the sidewalk to the other side of the street.

I was overwhelmed with anger and could not think of anything but destroying my own sons most vulnerable area, his backside.

I had gone halfway down the stairs to get a closer look at the situation and now, running back up the stairs, I rushed into our apartment.

I hurried pass Willie and went into the front room, opening the window facing the street. I leaned out of the window, scanning the ever growing crowd of onlookers.

I finally spotted my oldest son Buddie, and called to him loudly. I finally got his attention and told him to go and get his father from his job, that this was a real emergency.

In order to get outside and around to the front of the building, I had to go back through the apartment, and out the back door.

When I reached the kitchen, I snatched Willie up from the chair and out the back door we went.

As we were descending the stairs into the backyard, I

heard Sirens, Bells and Claxton horns blaring, mixed with the noise the still growing crowd was making.

As we advanced on the crowd up the street, a crowd that was now spilling up around the front of the building, and across the street in front of the restaurant and up the street. I got a firm grip on Willie's arm and glared at him, daring him to try and run.

We stepped into the crowd and walked across the street where we found space. With neighbors hanging out of their windows, yelling to the crowd, a police car and a Fire Engine pulled up, with the policemen now backing up the crowd in order to give the firemen room to work.

The crowd complied and backed up, now Willie and I were stuck in the middle of the crowd and had a good view of the front doorway.

By the time my son Buddie and my husband arrived, Willie and I were watching intently as the firemen tried to figure out a way to get the horse out of the doorway.

My husband and my son Buddie worked their way to our side, my husband pointing at the horses huge posterior protruding from the doorway. At that moment, the horse let out a loud fart and along with the crowd roaring, my husband was laughing harder than I'd seen him laugh in a long time.

I had to chuckle myself but quit right away when my husband, (Whose nick-name is Buster) saw me standing there, with a look of doom and gloom on my face.

He said, still chuckling, "OK! What's the big emergency?"

When I didn't answer him right away, he leaned over and whispered something into Buddies ear and pointed at the horses posterior. Which made Buddie double over with laughter.

Standing back up he looked at me saying, "So! What's the big emergency?"

Pointing at the rear end of the horse I said, "THAT! My dear husband is the big emergency!"

Buster gave me a perplexed look saying, "That?

The Horse? But! What has that got to do with us?"

As he thought, he looked around, the perplexed look turned into a frown of concentration. Just then there was a loud crash as the plate glass window in Sam Markowietz Grocery Store disintegrated.

The horse in its frustration and pain had flayed it's legs out, his rear hooves catching the metal seam, that held that section of the pane of glass together.

The glass exploded out in a shower as shards and bits of glass fell on some of the crowd, who were now pushing and shoving to get out of the way, but not wanting to get too far away from the scene.

I glared at Buster saying, "Now do you understand? I said, my voice angry, my frustration complete, "THERE!" My finger pointing at the now empty glass frame.

I said to buster, "Do you think that broken glass is funny? Well! See how much you'll be laughing when you have to pay for those panes of glass.

"See how much you'll be laughing when you have to pay for those panes of glass out of your own pocket, and you can bet, we're going to have to pay for those panes of glass." The smile left his face as he realized that I was not joking. He said quietly, more seriously, "What happened?

Where did that horse come from anyway? Who?. Who?

Wait-t-t-t-a- minute!" He suddenly looked around until his eyes fell on Willie. He said angrily, Willie! Did he make this mess?" The smile completely left his face, and both of us were looking pretty grim.

Buddie said, as he noticed Buster's change in demeanor, "What happened dad?"

I looked down at Willie, his now sweaty palm clasped tightly in my hand, saying angrily, "Yep! Willie has done it again.

"So you can just take your son up the back stairs, and while you're thinking about that broken window and how much it's going to cost us, you can more readily bring some pain to your son's rear end."

Letting go of Willie's hand, I pushed him over to where his father stood.

Buster rolled his eyes up to heaven and said in an exaggerated voice, "Ahh! So now he's MY son? Every time he does something wrong, which is almost all the time, he belongs to me right?"

He was looking at me with anger now in both his voice, and his face.

He was quiet for a moment but, then he expelled his breath and said, "Well, I don't blame you for passing the buck to me this time and believe me, the honors."

He turned to leave, holding Willie by the back of his shirt, near the back of his neck.

He stopped walking and turned back to me saying reflectively, "You know, this reminds me of the time Willie got his head caught in that steel barred fence on Belmont Avenue. You know! The fence that was around the Synagogue?"

He laughed quietly saying, "It took the Fire Department over an hour between arguing with the Rabbi, and prying the bars on the fence apart to free his big head."

He started to say something else but, gazed down at Willie, remembering where he was, and then he looked at the horses wide rear end, and the windows that were now gaping frames, glass all over the ground, and he got mad all over again, but shrugging his shoulders he said, "What the hell!"

The horse suddenly gave another painful scream and Busters face became a thunderstorm, as he took a firmer grip on Willies shirt and propelled him though the crowd saying, "Huh! You wait until I get you home boy! I bet you won't bring home an ant, no less a horse.

"Damned it boy! Leave it to you to do the impossible." But! as he and our son drew further and further away from me and Buddie, I could hear the slightest mellowness in his voice, as the humor of the situation seemed to be too much for him to hold back.

I saw him hustle Willie around the corner, his hand over his mouth as he tried to cover the fact that he was laughing.

As Buddie and I stood there watching the slow progress, as the firemen tried to figure out a way to get the horse out of the doorway.

Me hoping against hope that they would hurry and get him out, Buddie was enjoying the whole situation.

Frowning at Buddie, I motioned for him to follow me, and we set off taking the same route that Buster had taken with a completely frightened Willie.

By the time we got into the backyard, Policemen were going up to each apartment, getting statements from the occupants as to what they had seen.

Not wanting to talk to them until IIIII had a talk with Buster, so I hurried up the stairs with Buddie in front of me, into the backdoor of our apartment.

Entering, I expected to see Buster giving Willie either a serious talking to, or a serious whipping but, I didn't find them in my bedroom.

Going into the kitchen, I saw them sitting on the hallway stairs, watching as two firemen were greasing the horses bloated belly, while a third pulled and hauled on a harness that had been strapped on the horses back and rear.

The horse didn't like the harness and kicked the laboring fireman away. A roar went up from the crowd as they saw the fireman flying, making the policemen's job of containment that much harder, as they fought to keep the crowd from over-running the area and maybe getting completely out of hand.

There was a holiday spirit about the crowd as they stood around laughing, joking, and swapping the local news.

Feeling ashamed and mad at the same time, I tapped Buster on his shoulder, and motioned for him to follow me back into the apartment.

Once we were there, I pointed toward the boys bedroom, and he walked Willie into the bedroom and closed the door.

I waited for a few minutes and opened the door a crack.

I saw Buster waving a huge fist in Willies face, as the frightened boy sat on the edge of the bed. Buster was making faces and noises, and not really saying anything or doing anything.

I could sense the laughter bubbling just under the surface of Busters false anger, and my blood boiled that he wouldn't be more serious so, I decided on a plan of action of my own.

I led Buddie back out of the backdoor onto the porch.

We got halfway down the stairs and almost bumped into one of the policemen who was going around getting statements.

I stopped him and we went down stairs into the back-yard, where we stood and, starting from the beginning, I explained what had happened. He listened closely and took notes in a deft manner.

After I'd finished talking, he said, "Ma'am! The Fire Chief would like to speak to you.

"Now! If you'd bring your son Willie around the front of the building, I'm sure that the Chief will want to find out just how in the hell your son, got that damned horse to go into that hallway in the first place, as I'm sure that all of us would like to know.

Hell! It just ain't natural, because we are really catching it trying to get the horse out."

I must have been looking pretty scared because, he said quickly, "Don't worry Ma'am, everything's going to be alright, we're working on it and . . . ."

He saw that his words had no effect on me, and he said, "Lady! Look!" He said this with understanding in his voice, although there was hay-hem in his eyes.

"Ma'am, Just bring your son Willie down to the front of the building OK? If he could get that damned horse to go into that hallway, he just may have some kind-a idea as how we're gonna get that dad-burn animal out of that doorway."

Re-entering the rear of my apartment with Buddie in-tow, I saw that Buster had changed his attack methods, when I sat Buddie down in the kitchen and went up to the door of the boys bedroom.

Peeking through a crack in the door, I saw that Buster was now sitting on the edge of the bed, shaking his finger in Willie's face.

I said loudly, "What happened? Your fist got too heavy to hold up? So you had to exchange it for a finger?"

Buster looked up and said, "I was just explaining the facts of life to him and . . ."

I held out my hand saying, as I glared at my husband, "Willie! You come with me boy."

Leaving Buster sitting there with Buddie, I guided Willie out the backdoor saying as I left, "You talk to Buddie about the facts of life, after all, he's older than Willie.

Right now we don't have the time for a growing up lesson."

And I guided Willie down the stairs and up the street. The front of the building was a mess, with all of the onlookers, all of the police, and all of the firemen.

The onlookers yelling their encouragement to the Firemen, and roaring with laughter whenever the horse broke wind now and then.

Just as I was about to walk over to the Fire Chief, Buster walked up to my side. I said, "Where is Buddie?"

He said, "I left him with our neighbor Ethel. I figured that I had better be here in-case they try to do anything to Willie.

The mention of Willie's name, made me look around for him.

I found him hiding behind my skirts, quaking with fear. I said, "Stop trying to hide boy. You've done all the damage that you can possibly do."

Buster said, as we walked back toward the clot of people at the corner, "This ain't over yet, so don't talk so fast about Willie doing all the damage that he could possibly do."

He was now mumbling about wasting time off of his job, losing money that we needed. All the while, Willie was stumbling along trying to keep up with us.

When we turned the corner Buster said, "Hold on while I find the Fire Chief."

Walking around the edge of the crowd, he plunged into the crowd, disappearing from sight, as I got a tighter grip on Willie's hand, only to see Buster re-appear with the Fire Chief behind him.

The street was now packed with people almost to the middle of the block. The police had put up wooden horses to keep the crowd back.

The horse would scream in pain every once and a while, as it tried over and over to get unstuck from the door. Those screams stabbed at my heart. I promised that I would talk to Willie in depth about bringing animals home, ANY ANIMALS!"

When Willie saw Buster and the Fire Chief approaching us, he started pulling away trying to run but, I had a tight grip on his hand and Buster walked around behind us blocking any thought of Willie running away.

The Fire Chief squatted down in front of Willie and asked him in a soft and friendly voice, "Son, how did you get the hossie to follow you into the hallway?"

Willie was scared to death and just stood there, his mouth wide open, his fear making him sweat, his eyes like saucers, he couldn't talk.

Buster said angrily, "Speak up boy! We ain't got all day. I've got to get back to work, so speak up."

Willie blurted out, looking at me in absolute terror, "Mama! Don't let the man hurt me!'

The Fire Chief said, now loosing some of his patience, "Look Son! Time is very important, the hossie is getting tired, and is in a lot of pain, and we've got to get him out of that doorway.

So! I ask you, can you help us? We'll let you ride the Fire Truck if you do."

Buster said, the frustration of him having to just look on, as Willie just stood there crying, and just staring into the face of the Fire Chief, frowning back at him.

Buster said angrily, "Boy! You stop that noise RIGHT NOW! The man is talking to you so, stop that crying and answer him or I'll bust your backside wide open."

Willies tears dried up almost immediately, as another crash came from the area of where the horse was. The crowd surged back as more glass flew.

My heart sank a little further in my chest, as I knew that this last crash was the window of the storefront of the storefront on the other said of the hallway.

Getting a clear view of the horses very large back-

Side, as he flayed around and was kicking out the last fragments of the glass, blood now mixed with sweat, as the horse gained its footing and stood motionless, as the scattered firemen slowly creeped back close.

Buster said, as he started at the horse in the doorway, "You know, I've been thinking." He reached for Willie's hand and with one of his most determined looks said, "Come on boy!"

Without looking right or left, he brushed pass the Fire Chief, walking through the barricade that had been hastily thrown up, and walked pass the firemen, Policemen, who were taking a break, and waiting for more gear before giving it another try.

He led willie across the street toward the hallway door. When willie saw where they were going, he started trying to pull away, and screaming in fear, as the horses rear loomed high and wide before him.

The crowd had settled down and was watching intently as Buster, using one hand un-slung the straps that festooned the horses back, as with his other hand, he held Willie so that he couldn't run.

As soon as the straps fell away from the horses back and sides, Buster swung Willie up on the horses sticky, sweaty, greasy back, and called to the Police and Firemen to keep everybody back., that he was going to try something.

A single voice rose from the now quiet crowd saying, "Go Get um Buster! Go get um!'

The crowd roared with laughter, some whistling, and cheers, and I knew that it was Buster's cronies yelling their support.

I looked around at the crowd, and saw many people that we knew closely, and people we knew just to say hello to but,

I also knew that this story would be all over the neighborhood by nightfall.

The thought broke my humorous feelings because, I try to keep anything dealing with my family personal and close like everyone else does.

And up to this moment, I thought that I had done a good job of it. Now that Willie had done something stupid, we wouldn't have any peace for a while.

We'll really have to talk to both our sons once this is over.

Looking back at what was going on, I saw Buster as he walked around the side of the horses rear, motioning one of the firemen close he said something to him.

The firemen held Willie's leg as Buster disappeared around the corner. After a few minutes, we could hear Buster's voice coming out of the hallway.

Two more firemen hurried over as Buster was yelling out instructions.

The Fire Chief motioned for me to go over to the doorway. I hurried over and Buster said from inside the hallway, "Martha! Go up to the shop (His Job) and have him tell Tom and Barney to bring down a couple of jacks we have there to lift the backs of trucks with."

Without a word, I hurried up to Belmont Auto Springs where Buster worked, and I didn't have to look to hard for Tom and Barney, everyone had stopped working and was watching what was going on down the street. Only a few of the men going down to get a closer look.

So I found Tom and Barney on the fringe of the crowd and told them what Buster had said.

They hurried back up to the shop, yelling back at me that I should go back to where Buster was.

I hurried back and before I could get settled, Tom and Barney was walking pass me to the mouth of the hallway.

Laying the large jacks on the ground, Tom yelled into the hallway, "Buster! We brought three of the jacks. Are you alright?"

Buster answered, "Yea! Just leave the jacks with the firemen and thanks."

Tom said, "You'll have to tell us what happened when you get back to work."

Buster yelled, "Yea! I will."

Tom and Barney left and Buster called the firemen over to the doorway. One of them lifted Willie off of the horses back and handed him into the hallway where Buster's hands appeared for a moment and took Willie from the fireman.

The hands deposited Willie on the horses back near its neck.

The crowd seemed paused, and was totally quiet. Buster called out instructions to the firemen on how to hook up the jacks, because they were going to have to push the doorframe out some.

As the firemen worked with the jacks, the horse started to panic but, Buster was now petting the horse, rubbing it's neck and muzzle and Willie was petting the horse from his perch on it's neck.

After the firemen set the jacks, Buster instructed them to now put the straps back around the horses rear end.

After the straps were back in place, one fireman on the top jack, another on the bottom jack, and they both began a swinging motion as the jacks click notch after notch.

Soon the doorframe began to groan in protest but, began to widen the space around the horse middle, inch by inch.

Suddenly, there was a popping sound as the wood in the doorframe began to buckle under the pressure.

The crowd re-acted to every sound with oohs and ahh's but remained semi-quiet.

Suddenly, with the firemen tugging the teather straps from the street side, the horse now quiet, and the jacks resounding throughout the street, the horse began inching it's way backward out of the hallway.

As more and more of the horse could be seen, it's belly as bloated as ever, it gave a last blasting fart and was out.

Willie holding as much of its mane as he could get in his little hands, Buster holding the reins close at its muzzle guiding the animal.

The bottled up gas was free, as the horse continued breaking wind. Each time it broke wind, the crowd would roar with laughter.

The horse was skittish and whenever the crowd yelled, it would stiffen and tremble all over, but Buster's soft whispering and soothing voice, it just kept on backing out of the now broken doorway.

When the horse was finally out of the doorway, and had all four of it's hooves on solid pavement, a policeman guided it to the curb, where it's owner stood, a look of both anger and relief on his face.

This look of relief quickly disappeared and was replaced by one of shame, as the Fire Chief read him the riot act for leaving his horse unattended.

Telling him that he would be fined and would have to pay damages to Sam Markowietz (Who was both the landlord of the building, and the owner of the Grocery store, and the empty storefront beside it.)

A loud cheer arose from the crowd as Buster finally made an appearance. The police, the firemen, the crowd gave another mighty cheer when Buster waved at them.

One of Busters friends voices rose from the crowd, "OK Buster! Is this where you and little buster (That was what everyone called Willie) ride off into the sunset?"

The crowd roared, and started breaking up, going in different directions.

As I walked across the street to join Buster and Willie, some of the crowd that was still lingering surged forward and surrounded father and son.

I slowed my steps as I relived the moment of father and son working together. I saw the fear leave Willies face and be replaced with a calmness when he was seated on the horses neck.

I guess I'll always be a hopeless romantic because, I can swear I saw a joy in my son's face as he sat high above the crowd, and a sheer love of animals reflected from my husbands face as he guided the horse back to safety.

I quickly dabbed the tears from the corners of my eyes thinking, "It took a broken down plug horse to show me that under all of the bluster and sometimes bad temper of Buster's.

And under the devilish, prankish, hard headedness of Willie, were the same types of warm, loving human beings. I knew a moment of profound wonder at both father and son.

I said to myself in amazement, as I shook my head from side to side, and with great pride, "Will wonders never scease?"

THE END

THE BOMB

In the late 1940s Electronics Companies across the nation were trying to make a breakthrough, and the companies that today are making millions of dollars, were then in their infancy.

Based in a Newark, NJ suburbs, with its growing factory, was the Electronics Company, Inter-Tech, future Electronics, which had been operating since 1946.

They were hiring as many High School graduates as they could get to apply for a job there.

Andrew Jonathan Bell, the founder of the company, along with his three Associates, Peter Anthony Grey, Richard Aldwin Wainwright, and Roger Bradley Martin, felt positive that no minority would ever be working in their facility or ever trying for a position.

If a minority were to even accidentally venture into their facility, in answer to ads in the local newspaper.

The four Executives felt that they had a back-up plan that

would stop any blacks, or lower class whites, Puerto Ricans or any other minority from applying.

The companies secretarial pool had been alerted, and whenever one of 'Those people' came to apply for a job, they were given the task of having to complete a project that Mr. Bell and his Associates had left incomplete on purpose.

Mainly because they couldn't complete the project themselves, and felt that if they couldn't complete it, then surely, regardless of his Academic standing, no minority could ever complete it.

But this way, the undesirable youths filling out the applications, and taking the test, couldn't say that they had not been given a 'fair' chance to land a job at this up scaled factory.

One day, in 1947, a young man named Ralph Addison, freshly graduated from South Side High School in Newark, NJ's black community, walked through the doors of Inter-Tech Electronics, seeking a job.

When the young man picked up an application and sat down at one of the desks in the main lobby, he looked around the room and saw that all of the young men sitting there filling out applications, were white, and had stopped writing, and were looking at him with a look of disdain on their faces.

Not seeming to be intimidated by the stares, he smiled at their discomfort to himself, and began filling out the application, ignoring the rest of the room.

The secretary, a slender blond, with cornflower blue eyes,

and a soft voice, was also staring at the youth, her face full of mixed emotions. Standing up in the tension filled room, she walked over to the desk the youth was occupying, and said in almost a whisper, "How old are you boy?"

The young man looked up from his application and said, a smile on his face, that didn't quite reach his dark brown eyes, "I'm sixteen years old Ma'am! Oh! And I know I look young but I . . ."

The secretary said, a firm note in her voice, "Are you sure you're in the right place? Shouldn't you be in school with the rest of the teenagers?"

He said, in a voice that was slightly annoyed, "I graduated from High School last week Eh . . . .Ma'am."

She hesitated momentarily sidetracked by his answer and, trying to regain the upper foot in this conversation she said, "Eh! . . . regardless of your age, I'm sure that you've stumbled into the wrong building.

"And would do better in a job that's suited to a boy of your age. Such as perhaps a grocery store, or a stock boy of some kind?"

Instead of being dismayed by what the secretary said, he smiled and said, "Strange that you should mention it but, those were exactly the jobs that I was offered."

He explained to the secretary that he was searching for a job that would be more challenging, rather than the regular jobs offered in his Local Community. Such as grocery store clerk, stock boy in a department store, Shoe Store, a Haberdashery, or a Hat Shop.

Still looking up at the secretary, the smile leaving his face as an annoyed look now turned into one of impatience as he tried to explain his reasoning, he said, "The only reason I came here was because I was tired of trying to get a job near where I live.

"And after coming across that ad in the Newark Star Ledger, stating that you were accepting applications, I decided to apply.

"The idea of working in electronics appealed to me! EH! . . . . Ma'am."

The secretary said as she quickly scanned the application, paying more attention to him, "But you're so young! And I . ."

Suddenly her boss Mr. Bell, who was walking through, stopped in front of them saying quietly in her ear, "Is there a problem Miss Johnson?"

At a strapping 6'3" and about 235 lbs, Mr. Bell stood towering over the seated youth. He wore his hair in a crew cut, he had a high forehead, bushy eyebrows that tended to flare out and give him a stoic demeanor that made his demeanor rather harsh, and unbreakable, which usually fooled any one unaware of his true thoughts and ideas.

His hazel eyes blazed over his roman nose with its flaring nostrils, and sat over lips that had a determined set to them.

The clef in his chin gave power to his face, and he used

his size and voice to overpower any adversary and it usually worked.

Miss Johnson started to speak, when Mr. Bell motioned for her to follow him. In front of her desk, he said in a whisper, "What are you trying to do? Get us put out of business? Just when we're finally gaining the confidence of these locals? And are appealing to the youth of this community?"

A look of fear came to the secretaries face as she said, "But Sir! He just walked in and . . . ."

Mr. Bell grabbing the secretary by her arm, and rushing her out of the room, the young man's application gripped tightly in her hand.

As soon as they were in Mr. Bell's office, he got on the Inter-Com and said, "Peter! You, Rick, and Roger get in here Pronto!"

Once his associates were seated in his office, Mr. Bell said, "Gentlemen! We've got us a problem."

Rick said idly, "Problem? What kind of problem."

Mr. Bell said, looking at Miss Johnson as though whatever was wrong was her fault, "There's a young black boy sitting in the lobby applying for a job and instead of following the script, she stood there questioning him."

Glaring at the young woman, he said to her, "That boy should have been in and out of there within a matter of minutes."

Peter said, "Ah! If she seems to be having a problem

with this kid, then all she has to do is just accept the kids application and then toss it in the trash after he leaves.

"Then have her call him in a couple of days saying that you've already hired someone to fill the slot he was applying for."

Mr. Bell said, "Yes! I could have her do that. Besides, hes under age."

Roger said angrily, "And remember, he's black! Now you tell me, what would a black person know about Electronics? So! Don't even waste any-more time with this kid."

Mr. Bell said, "WAIT!" With a sly grin on his face, he said, "Let's have some fun with this kid, at his own expense."

Roger said, "What do you have in mind?" A smirk on his face.

Mr. Bell said, "I think we should trot out the 'BOMB ' and show the blacks that young or old, we won't tolerate them even trying to muscle in on our jobs."

Miss Johnson looked at her boss with admiration in her eyes, as all four of the men laughed.

Peter said, "Don't you think that the BOMB would be a little too sophisticated for a kid.?"

Roger said, "Why Not! Kid or Grownup, this way we'll get rid of the people we don't want.

"You know? The lower IQ types that now and then try to break through.

"The blacks have been trying from the first day, maybe

once we send this boy packing, then maybe they'll get the message."

Mr. Bell said, "It's sad that we have to make an example out of such a fine looking young boy but! As long as we can eliminate him quickly, I don't see any harm being done, but we can always say that we gave him a chance."

A satanic smile on his face.

Looking at Miss Johnson with grim eyes, he said, "But! we must treat him with the same civility that we treat anyone else, you must remember that."

Roger said, consternation in his voice, "But why must we . . ."

Mr. Bell said, "You see? That's why I'm the one that founded this company." Pointing to his temple he said, "It's because I think more about the future than the present, or the past."

Rick said, angry at the insinuation, "What's that! suppose to mean?"

Mr. Bell said, his change of direction quite obvious, "It means that even as poor as the blacks are, they will be buying our products themselves one day.

"So! Instead of just showing the kid the door, we at least give him a shot at 'THE BOMB ', Stating innocently that we could not complete this project and that all of the applicants have the same chance at a job here, by taking on the project with a two week deadline to complete it."

Miss Johnson said, a slight edge in her voice, "But! he's

only fifteen years old, and I think that what you're intending to do to a little kid I . . ."

Cutting her off, and looking around the room with a smirk on his face, he continued by saying, "When this young man realizes that he can't possibly complete the 'BOMB', he can't say that we didn't give him a fair chance at the job, and he'll seek his fortunes somewhere else."

Looking around the quiet room again, all he saw was satisfied smiles. Standing up, a signal that the meeting was over, Mr. Bell sent Miss Johnson back to her desk with orders to bring the young man back to his office in ten minutes, giving him and his Associates time to set up the 'BOMB.' In the Lobby, Ralph Addison sat nervously at his desk and began losing his patience, as many of the young men sitting there with her began disappearing into the rear offices for interviews.

Impatient at the long wait, he was about to stand up and leave, when Miss Johnson returned.

She didn't have his application in her hand, and this gave him pause, so gritting his teeth, he sat back down.

Miss Johnson sat at her desk and after giving Ralph a curious glance, she busied herself by gathering up applications, calling out names on them and directing the young men back to the different offices for interviews.

Finally, after what seemed like forever to the boy, he saw Miss Johnson speak quietly into the Inter-Comm and stand up, motioning for him to follow her.

She led him to Mr. Bell's office, a smile on her lips as she thought about what her boss was going to do.

This would REALLY be something to share over lunch with the rest of the secretary's. She tittered to herself as she disappeared back into the lobby, leaving the boy at Mr. Bells office door.

Mr. Bell Opened his door and ushered him into his office saying, "Come in son, and please, have a seat."

Ralph Addison looked around the office and his eyes fell on the table. Just at that moment, Mr. Bell said, "Ahh! I see you've noticed exactly what I had you brought here for."

Walking from behind his desk he said, "Come over here son." And he led Ralph over to the table.

On the table was 'THE BOMB' an Electronics nightmare that would have stymied the best of young men, because it had come to a sudden halt when Mr. Bell and his Associates couldn't find the one Component and set of numbers that would complete the project. In other words, it even stymied it's inventors.

Mr. Bell and his Associates explained what was there to the boy as he stood in front of the table, and explained just how far they had advanced and where they stopped.

Not speaking, or looking nervous, the young man looked at the project with an intense focused eye, as Mr. Bell explained what him and his Associates thought he would have to do to continue, and possibly complete the Project.

The young man never said a word throughout the

dissertation, his face mixed with an excitement that he'd never felt before.

He was sent on his way with four long narrow tubes of schematics under his arm, a brand new T-Square, and a few other measuring tools, along with a fourteen day deadline. Sure that this was just another person who they could blow off, although Mr. Bell felt a small sense of guilt at the apparent youthfulness of this boy.

One of his Associates laughed saying, ruthlessly, "Regardless of his age, the boy should learn early in life, that angels fear to tread where fools rush in, and then we should be able to get back to business as usual in not time."

Picking up the wrinkled application from his desk, Mr. Bell balled it up and dropped it into the wastebasket and lightly dusted off his hands, all without once looking at it.

Miss Johnson was told to be on the lookout for the young man's return. This time with frustration and resignation on his face and in his body language.

Four days later, young Ralph Addison walked back through the front doors of Inter-Tech Electronics, the four tubes under his right arm and all of the measuring tools still stuffed in the same large envelope he had tucked under his left arm, and a more pronounced assurance in his bearing.

He stepped up to the secretary's desk, asking to speak to Mr. Bell. And although she was surprised at his manner, she tried to pretend that his request was of no consequence and shrugging, she spoke into the Inter-Comm and shortly after that, Mr. Bell appeared, a condescending smile on his face. A smile that vanished when he saw the genuine smile and the assured manner in his body language, he glanced nervously at the four tubes under the young man's arm, he said, in a somewhat flustered voice, "Please! Come with me."

All of the applicants had stopped filling out their applications, to watch this show of false warmth toward the black youth.

And as the two disappeared towards Mr. Bell's office. Disgruntle mutterings could be heard from the applicants, who's eye's followed the two all the way to Mr. Bells office.

He ushered the young boy into his office, his Associates now sitting in wait, the same fixed smiles on all of their faces as Mr. Bell said, giving them a knowing look, "It seems that you have shown up quite a bit earlier than any of our other job seekers who undertook the task of trying to solve the 'BOMB.'

"What happened? Did you find that it was a little too much?" Motioning with his hand he said, "Please! Have a seat. Do you want coffee? Or a soft drink?"

A look of impatience flashed across the young boy's face and was gone quickly, as he vaguely smiled and declined any refreshments as his eyes followed Mr. Bell around behind his desk.

Once Mr. Bell had seated himself, young Addison Stood back up and as though he had been waiting for this moment, he laid the four tubes on the table, opening up the large envelope and taking out the T-Square and pointing to them, he simply said, "What else do you have?"

Mr. Bell said in a puzzled voice, "What do you mean?"

The young boy said in clipped tones, "It's finished! Done!"

The office was deadly quiet as Mr. Bell said, a look of disbelief on his face, "Surely you're joking?"

Looking around the room at his Associates, who also had a look of disbelief on their faces as he said, "But you couldn't have."

The young boy opened the first and longest tube and shaking out the schematics, walked over and spread it out on the table.

He then pulled a slide rule out of the inside pocket of his jacket, and began explaining the different equations he had used to come to his conclusions.

After emptying the rest of the tubes on the table, he showed the four men where they had gone awry in their calculations, and how he had amended their notations on the schematics, to either add information or subtract information not needed.

Speaking with eloquent convictions for one so young, when he had finished explaining how he had come to his conclusion, all four of the schematics were spread out on the table.

The young man said in closing, "I took the liberty of incorporating some of my own ideas into your schematics, without them you would probably be another two or three years trying to complete this project."

Sitting down, he beamed all four of the men an energetic smile saying, "I enjoyed the challenge, so! What else do you have?" As he slid the slide rule back into his jacket pocket.

The four men sat there in their Brooks Brothers Suits, and their Stacy-Adams shoes, a look of sheer bewilderment on their faces, as they looked at the young black boy sitting in front of them, in his hand-me-down jacket and slacks, his cheap white shirt, and his Thom McCan shoes.

Yet he wore his clothes as though they were as well tailored as the men sitting around him.

After a long pause, Mr. Bell said to the boy, a note of conviction in his voice, "Go to Miss Johnson's desk and get another application.

Take it home and fill it out, writing in anything you might have left out of your first application, and bring it back tomorrow morning, nine O'Clock sharp.

"You're hired!! And will be working out of my office." The young man stood up thanking them, and left the office.

Once the young boy was gone, Mr. Bell hurried and got a slide rule out of his desk draw, and began rechecking all of the young man's quotients, as his Associates gathered around him.

Once all four of the men were seated again, Mr. Bell said, "Gentlemen! We've just been upstaged by a boy, and a black boy at that."

Slamming his fist on his desk he said, a note of exasperation in his voice, as he said in disgust, "And I took him for granted, never looking at his application, and I'm sure that Miss Johnson didn't really look at his application either."

Rick said, a note of anxiety in his voice, "Wait! What you said about this boy being hired, you didn't really mean that did you? If you did, then what were you thinking?"

Mr. Bell said, to no one in particular, "I don't know what I'm thinking right now."

Completely flabbergasted, he said to the ceiling, "How could he have come up with the answers he did? And him a mere youngster!" The last said with a small sense of awe in his voice.

Peter said, "What did you do with his application? Let's take a look at if."

Mr. Bell said, Sarcasm heavy in his voice, "If you'll remember, I threw it in the trash can, thinking that his being black, poor, and a very young boy, he would be overwhelmed by both the 'BOMB' and by the fact that he was up against the establishment, therefore, not stand a chance to get a job here."

He continued by saying, "But! He seems well spoken and even though being black, and quite naïve, he seems to have more understanding and intelligence about what we are doing here, than most of the whites who are applying here, Adults, and Young Adults.

"And at the end of the day, it all boils down to a matter

of brains and exactly how far we want this company to go doesn't it?

"Do we want to pass up a chance to benefit from a boy who is undisputedly a genius, or do we want to forego and opportunity to make millions. . . . NO! Billions, because we're bigots?"

When there was no response from his now disgruntled Associates, he said, "Well, I'm not ready to let this young boy take his gifts to some other company and make them rich. Ohh! NOo! Not on your life."

The timbre of his voice told his Associates that he had made his decision, when he said, "Gentlemen! I think we're going to have to make an exception of the rules, in regard to this young boy."

Getting on the Inter-Com before there could be any negativity from his Associates, he said, "Miss Johnson, as soon as that Youngman Ralph Addison brings his application back tomorrow morning, having him wait out there and serve him whatever he wants. But! bring his application directly to my office."

Miss Johnson said in a slightly caustic voice, "But Sir! There will be applicants here waiting for interviews and some will be filling out applications, and . . ."

Mr. Bell said, his voice taking on measured tones, "Deal with this Miss Johnson, Deal with it."

Peter said, "You mean, you're actually thinking of hiring

this . . . This, OooH NO! Forget it! We cannot have any blacks working here.

Do you realize that hiring this kid would open the floodgates and our company would be finished almost before it got started?"

Looking off into the distance, the anger and distaste stark on his face, he continued by saying, "Just think about it, a Black Assed . . ."

Mr. Bell said grimly, "Peter! Peter! We've been friends for a very long time. And you're good at your job, but! Please get pass that racist attitude long enough to realize just how important this decision is.

"I cannot make you change your mind, nor your basic roots of hatred of these people, and if that's how it will be, then so be it, although, I'm sure you're exaggerating the whole situation.

"But! I won't let race get in the way of business and, gentlemen! Believe me, this is now about business.

I won't ignore the fact that a mere boy reversed the affects, of the 'BOMB.'

"Having! what turned out to be a childish prank from the beginning, blow up in our faces, with exceptional ease, from an exceptional kid."

Looking around the now quiet room, and seeing that his words had struck home, he continued by saying, "In a way, we're more fortunate than a lot of out competitors."

Peter said, "And how is that?"

Mr. Bell said, explaining the situation, as he would to a child, "The other companies usually get the same types that we get.

"The smart asses that feel a right to passage, and are far to over-confident that they will get the job simply because they are white.

"And then there's the ones that are older and really have nothing new to contribute, and the other companies turn away blacks without finding out if they are smart or dumb.

"Now! This young man? He's not taking anything for granted and truly takes the job seriously.

"Do you realize that he could generate ideas that could revolutionize our company? And isn't that what we're in business for? Brand New Ideas in Electronics?

"And most of all, Profits! And Gentlemen, Profits takes precedent over whatever race this boy is."

—ɯ—

The next morning, young Ralph Addison walked through the doors of Inter-Tech Electronics at nine O'clock sharp.

Handing Miss Johnson his application, he walked over and sat down beside three white men, who gave him a curious glance, as Miss Johnson hurried to Mr. Bell's office with the boys job application in her hand.

When she returned to her desk, she said to Ralph Addison, "Will you have Coffee? Or perhaps a soft drink? Pr - perhaps you would like a bagel with cream cheese?"

The young boy said, "No thanks, I'm fine."

After a few minutes, Miss Johnson guided the boy to Mr. Bell's office. After she had retreated back to her desk, the three Associates sat looking at the young boy as Mr. Bell sat behind his desk reading the application.

Mr. Bell was surprised to note that Ralph Addison had Graduated with Honors, at the head of his class and had skipped two grades in Junior High School, and a grade in High School.

His greatest strength was the fact that he had an IO of 187, which was a bit above genius, and although he was adept in most areas, Math was his crowning Glory.

He clicked on the Inter-Com saying to Miss Johnson, "You can take your morning break now. Hell! Take an extra Fifteen Minutes, and you can send the young men here for me to interview home, and tell them to return in a couple of days."

Turning to the young boy with new eyes, he realized that even in a room full of white executives, the boy wasn't intimidated in the least.

Looking around his office, Mr. Bell said to his Associates, "Remember Gentlemen, profits takes precedent over whatever race this boy is."

Looking at the faces of his spellbound Associates, Mr. Bell thought to himself, 'This is what sets me three, or four rungs up the ladder from you guys.

"You live on with your petty prejudices, and in the end

I'll look at the overall picture, and think of what's REALLY good for my company in the long run.'

The top Executives at Inter-Tech Electronics were learning the true meaning of the old adage, 'Never judge a book by its cover.'

Mr. Bell finally said, handing the application to Rick, "Gentlemen! Meet our new trainee, Mr. Ralph Addison."

He sat quietly watching as his Associates passed the application from one to the other, a wide grin on his face, a grin that was for once genuine.

After Mr. Bells Associates read the application, they looked at the youth with new eyes, Peter saying, "But! Remember, he's only fifteen years old. How will we get around that?"

Rick said, "You must remember, he's being hired as a trainee, and that can last for as long as we deem it necessary."

Standing up, Mr. Bell walked around his desk and shook the youth's hand, saying, "Welcome to Inter-Tech Electronics."

As his three associates lined up to shake the youths hand, Ralph Addison said, "Thank you for giving me this chance.

"I will now be able to do more than dream about the many things that are in my head. Things that I can possibly contribute to your company."

Mr. Bell said, "You can report to work in two days, we have to set up an office for you to work out of."

As young Ralph Addison walked out of Inter-Tech Electronics that day, he could feel the resentment but, when he thought of the things he would be doing, his sense of excitement heightened his and his resolve to succeed.

In the end, he would show them all, that there really isn't any difference in people except that there are smart ones, and dumb one's, and color has nothing to do with it, or was he just being naïve?

THE END

THE CELEBRITY

While lounging out on the ramp, behind the Ambassador Hotel, in the Atlantic City, New Jersey of 1958, waiting to go to work.

The time was 4: O'clock in the afternoon and my being unusually early, and being a dishwasher in one of the two huge kitchens in the hotel, I wasn't too anxious to go to work, and I knew that if I was spotted, they would want me to go to work ASAP.

So! while waiting where I knew I wouldn't be noticed, smoking and leaning against the building.

Looking up and down the desolate street, my eyes came to rest on the figure of a man standing at the foot of the Ramp, right beside the curb, with a large amount of luggage surrounding him. Curious, I ambled down the ramp, which was very long, stopping in front of the man, figuring to keep him company until his ride came.

As I approached him, I saw that he wore one of those Swiss Alpine hats, and was neatly dressed in a pair of dove colored slacks, a white silk shirt open at the collar, a brown tweed sports jacket, and medium brown loafers.

When I reached him, he smiled and said in a soft voice, "Hi! How are you?"

Something about his voice stirred a note of familiarity. I had heard his voice before and he looked Familiar but, I couldn't place the face. So I said out of curiosity, "I'm fine . . Eh! Do you have a problem?" I had noticed that he kept looking at his watch and swept the street with his eyes, a slight annoyed expression on his face.

He said, as he looked at his watch again, "Yes! I do seem to have a problem of sorts. My man Friday hasn't shown up and I have to get this luggage across the street and on the ramp of that Hotel across the street because, that's where I'll be staying tonight." I said, "Oh! You're changing Hotels."

He gave me an impatient look, saying, "No! I'm not changing Hotels. I'll be starring in this Hotel tomorrow night, but! I have to stay in that Hotel."

Not wanting him to get any more upset, I said quickly, "Is that all?"

Looking up and down the still deserted street, I said, "I can help you there, hang on, I'll be right back."

I hustled back up the ramp and went inside the rear of the Hotel where they kept large dolly's and rolled one out on the ramp, rolling it down the ramp I brought it to rest beside the mound of luggage and we started loading it on the dolly.

Once we had it all loaded on the dolly, we both pulled it

across the street to the rear of the Hotel on the opposite side of the street, and he went around and got up on the delivery platform, where I handed up the luggage to him.

All the while I was handing up the luggage I had a Gnawing feeling in my gut that I knew this man from somewhere but, dismissed the thought for the moment.

We finally got all of the luggage up on the platform and he came down to where I was standing and said, "I really appreciate this." As he spoke, he brought out his wallet. Feeling slightly offended I said, "No! That's alright!"

He said, "But I want to give you a little something for . . . . !"

I said, "No! That's alright, I did it because you needed help, not because I was looking for a payday, your thanks is enough."

Looking at my watch I said, "I have to get to work now."

He smiled saying, "Look! Since you won't accept any money, here!" He handed me a card saying, "If you ever need ANYTHING! You just call this number. Eh! . . What's your name?

I said, "My name is Bill He wrote my name down in a black address book he had taken from his pocket.

Putting the address book back in his pocket he said, "Remember! If you need anything, call me."

I started to leave but hesitated saying, "You know! There is one thing!"

He said, "Yes?"

I said, "For some strange reason, I feel like I know you from somewhere, have we ever met before?"

He smiled and said, "No! I've never seen you before but, I'm sure you've seen me before."

Holding out his hand, he shook my hand saying, "I'm NAT KING COLE."

While I rolled the dolly back across the street, I noticed that the street was still deserted.

Turning back for one last look, I saw the celebrity now giving instructions to a bellhop as to what to do with his luggage. I felt awed and uplifted by the experience, and never forgot it.

THE END

Printed in the United States
By Bookmasters